I0546507

TIME AND FOREVER

SUSAN B. JAMES

Dreams R Us Publishing

Los Angeles

TIME AND FOREVER

Copyright©2014

SUSAN B. JAMES

Second Edition 2024

Cover Design by Fiona Jayde.

This book is a work of fiction. The names, characters, places, and incidents are the products of the author's imagination or are used fictitiously. Any resemblance to actual events, business establishments, locales, or persons, living or dead, is entirely coincidental.

All rights reserved. No part of this publication may be reproduced, stored in a retrieval system, or transmitted in any form or by any means (electronic, mechanical, photocopying, recording, or otherwise) without the prior written permission of both the copyright owner and the publisher. The only exception is brief quotations in printed reviews.

Published in the United States of America by Dreams R Us Publishing

Los Angeles CA

Print ISBN 978-1-7370751-7-2

Ebook ISBN 978-1-7370751-6-5

To my sister, Kelly Dowell.

Thanks for being my biggest fan.

Acknowledgements

This book was made possible by the love and encouragement of a lot of people.

First a huge thank-you to Chris Baty and company for creating NaNoWriMo — National Novel Writing Month. .

To Kelley Armstrong for my first professional critique.

To Lynda Burch for pointing out flaws I needed to correct.

To Cheryl Yeko for finding merit in the story and suggesting vital changes.

To my beloved Pen and Inkers: Lupe Fernandez, Hilde Garcia, and Kris Kahrs who allowed me to take the story through our children's book critique group and who made the manuscript much better.

To Nancy Stewart for the gift of a line edit. I owe you big-time, Nancy.

Chapter 1

"Birthdays bite," Sherry muttered.

"Hey, in two more years you'll be sixty-five." Lorena raised her glass. "Here's to Medicare. The best present ever."

"Cute." Sherry stabbed Mr. Chow's chicken satay with an ebony chopstick. "Do you ever feel like something's missing in your life?"

"All the time." Lorena expertly chopsticked a mixed water dumpling. "This morning I found my car keys in the fridge under the cottage cheese."

"I'm not talking about senior moments. Heaven knows I have enough of them. I meant do you ever feel you should be taking another path?"

Lorena glanced around the celebrity-filled restaurant. "Jen Aniston's waving at you. She probably wants to know why *Now and Then* is closed."

Sherry returned Jen's finger wave. "Halloween tapped us out. We have to restock."

Lorena smiled back at Meg Ryan. "Ever since that piece on Entertainment Tonight you and your vintage clothing store are more popular than me, and I'm the celebrity." She offered Sherry a dumpling. "Why would you take another path? You're rich, thin, and you've got a great business. What else do you need?"

"Someone to share it with. I don't want to spend the rest of my life alone."

For a moment Lorena's eyes looked empty. She blinked and the mask returned. "There's a lot to be said for being alone. You get to eat crackers in bed and you have total control of the remote. If you're lonely, get a dog."

"I feel like there has to be more." Sherry cursed herself for making Lorena think of David and changed the subject. "I got a birthday card from Brittany and Bill."

Lorena's eyes frosted over. "How are the Bimbo and the Bore? Still wildly in love with each other."

"Yeah," Sherry said morosely. "They want to get together for dinner."

"Sherry, I get you staying on good terms with Bill for the boys' sake, but dinner *à trois* is going way beyond the call of duty. Tell them you have a date with George Clooney and you're too busy to bother."

"Yeah. Right." Sherry inhaled the marzipan aroma of her Almond champagne. Normally she never had a second glass, but it was her birthday and she loved the feel of the bubbles tickling down her throat and forming a pool of liquid courage in her stomach. "You know what? I'm tired of having the only male companionship in my life come from daydreams and romance novels. I want to be loved by a real person. I'm thinking of trying online dating."

"Are you *crazy*?"

Sherry rolled her eyes. "I knew you'd say that."

Lorena's sharp tone attracted the attention of the diners at the next table. "Look! It's Marley, the secretary on *Looking for Love*," the woman informed her companion. She beamed at Lorena. "Hi, Marley."

Lorena flipped back her streaked blonde bob, and gave the tourists her trademark ditzy smile.

Both women lifted their phones for a picture.

Lorena turned back to Sherry and continued in a lower voice. "You just cued the horror movie music in my head. When it comes to clichés, online dating is right up there with the *let's investigate* moment where the heroine takes the flashlight and runs around the creepy house in the dark."

"That's ridiculous." Sherry tried to lift one eyebrow and failed. "Lots of people are finding great matches online."

Lorena shuddered. "Lots of people are not you. Honey, look at yourself. You've got lollipop green eyes and a sweet smile that says *Take me. I'm vulnerable.* You'd be Little Red Riding Hood inviting in the Wolf."

"Stop that!" Sherry hated fairytale comparisons. She'd been dealing with them her whole life. "You're putting me off and I want to be encouraged. I want a chance at true love."

Lorena passed her hands over her glass. "I am looking into the future and I see . . . You and a Corgi. It's a perfect match."

"I don't want a dog, I want a human," Sherry retorted.

"I don't get it. You've gone twenty years without anyone. Why now."

"I was okay alone when I still had the boys at home, but now . . ." Sherry's smile wobbled. "Now there's no one to hug me anymore. I miss being touched." She saw the echo of pain in Lorena's eyes. Damn! She'd done it again. Sherry downed the rest of her champagne. "The kids are off having their adventures. It's time I had an adventure of my own."

"Why don't you start with a *little* adventure? One which doesn't involve the risk of coming home in a body bag." Lorena pulled out her iPhone. "There's this place Darien, my trainer, told me about called, The Castle. They've got themed restaurants, but their specialty is virtual reality adventures."

Sherry shook her head. "I'm not into video games."

Lorena called for the check. "Me neither, but Darien says this is different. It's a virtual world. And while you're in it, you have the ability to walk around, eat food, buy stuff, and do pretty much anything you would do in your actual life." She looked at the email on her iPhone. "*A world that seems so real, you won't believe it's virtual,*" she quoted.

"What kind of world?"

"Whatever you want, I guess. Darien said he and Carl picked Los Angeles in the eighties."

"Now that's just gross. Nobody in their right mind would revisit the eighties." Sherry took the iPhone and studied the email on the screen. "Any era? You know where I'd love to go? London, 1969."

"Why?"

"It was my first adventure. I had a job with the Marketing Exchange for six months. London was so alive and I loved the clothes and the music, and . . ."

Lorena leaned forward. "How 'bout the people? Any special person?"

Sherry felt her face flush. She couldn't tell Lorena about Jeremy. What would she say? *I once kissed a total stranger on the tube. And it was magical.* "There almost was, but it didn't come to anything." She handed the phone back to Lorena. "I'm in. Let's go to the sixties." A bubble of fun coursed through her. Or was it the champagne? "Two grown women going on a VR adventure. You think this is the first sign of second childhood?"

"Honey, I never finished with my first." Lorena scribbled her autograph on the check. "Come on, let's go."

Chapter 2

Lorena turned into a driveway lined with derelict sound stages near the Burbank airport.

"You're kidding right?" Sherry looked around, disbelieving. "Let's go to my house and check out eHarmony."

"Patience, my little chicken."

The driveway curved around to the rear. The back wall of the sound stage was faced in crenellated stone and looked like the entrance to a castle.

"This is amazing. You'd never guess from the front. Wait . . ." Sherry stared at the beautiful woman dressed in 1940s Dior coming out of the front door. "Isn't that Scarlett Johansson?"

"Probably. It's one of those *in* secrets. It's not listed and they don't advertise." Lorena handed her keys to the valet. "You have to know someone to get the number. Darien gave it to me in exchange for an introduction to my agent. Lord knows how he got it."

The red uniformed doorman opened the massive wooden door and bowed them into the front room. The scent of tuberoses from the huge flower arrangement reminded Sherry of the Bel Air Hotel lobby. Except for the red Chinese wallpaper.

"It looks like the entry to Disney's Haunted Mansion," Lorena said.

Sherry agreed.

Two large rooms opened off the main hall. One resembled a Victorian restaurant. A Strauss waltz wove through the buzz of conversation and the clink of silverware.

The other room was Art Deco with a sleek modern bar. A Charlie Chaplin film played on a flat screen TV. The voice of Billie Holliday crooned, "What Is This Thing Called Love?"

The tuxedoed Concierge came forward. "Good evening. Two for dinner?"

Lorena flashed her Marley smile. "I was told you specialize in VR adventures."

"Of course. Right this way, Marley." His fair skin reddened. "Ah . . . Sorry. Ms. Anderson." He led them through a hallway lit with faux candles and opened a door with an ornate sign: *Choose Your Adventure.* "You start here. Enjoy!"

"This room looks like a warehouse," Lorena said, pitching her voice to be heard over the machines thrumming in the background. Framed travel posters relieved the starkness of the institutional green walls. "It sounds like *War Games* in here."

The surfer boy behind the desk looked up and grinned at them. "Yeah. It takes a huge computer to handle this program. Hi, I'm Eric." He pointed to the menu on the wall. "Where would you like to go?"

Sherry didn't bother to look at the menu. "Can we do London in 1969?"

Eric's fingers flew over the keyboard. "May I please see your credit cards?"

Sherry opened her purse.

Lorena put her hand over Sherry's. "My treat. Happy Birthday." She handed Eric her American Express.

He inserted it into a white box attached to the computer. It lit up and spat out two plastic cards and a sheaf of paper. He stapled several together and handed a thick packet to Lorena. "Here you go."

Sherry peered over Lorena's shoulder. "Those look like the travelers checks I bought when I went to London."

Eric nodded. "That's the way you use them."

"Nice touch," Lorena commented. "Makes you feel like you're going back in time."

Eric smiled and pointed at another door. "Follow the floor lights and be kind to the natives."

Sherry stepped inside the darkened hallway. "Interesting ambiance." Pink neon daisies danced a pattern on the floor, blinking on and off to the throbbing, whisper filled music. "I know this song, but I can't remember the name of it."

Lorena hummed a couple of bars. "Time of The Season" by The Zombies. I had an old boyfriend who loved it. That's one of the reasons we broke up."

"Do I want to know the other reasons?"

"No. You don't."

They followed the daisies. Dim sounds came from behind unmarked doors lining the hallway. *"It's the time of the season when the love runs high . . ."* echoed and danced to the daisies. The daisy lights stopped at one of the unmarked doors and wove a pattern over it.

Sherry spotted a card slot and inserted her ticket. "Here goes nothing." The slot blinked green. The door opened into a dimly lit, narrow walled room with a second door at the far end.

A pleasant computer voice greeted them. "Please enter. There will be a brief wait while your experience is programmed."

Lorena looked at Sherry and shrugged. "Nothing ventured . . . Come on."

Sherry followed Lorena. The door swung closed. A blue light traveled up and down their bodies. The light snapped with a bright flash, followed by a stomach churning sensation like an elevator dropping too fast.

"Oh my god, what was that?" Sherry clung to Lorena. "An earthquake?"

"Don't think so. I never felt dizzy in an earthquake. My head feels weird." Lorena sounded spooked. "Let's get out of here."

A second door swung open. They stepped through it. They appeared to be on a street in London. Young men in Teddy suits sported Beatle haircuts. Girls with long straight hair strode along in knee high boots. A blast from a horn broke the thrum of traffic as a whizzing Vespa cut off a red double-decker bus.

Lorena stopped in the doorway. "Darien was right. Virtual Reality's come a long way,"

"It certainly looks like 1969." Sherry took a deep breath. The smells. Sausages and chestnuts. Autumn air and petrol. "How do they do this?"

"Darien thought it was derived from a military platform used for pre-Iraq training." Lorena scrutinized the passersby. "I'm guessing they use actors. He said the merchandise and the food were definitely real."

Sherry turned to Lorena and froze. "Lorena?" The girl in front of her had Lorena's eyes, but her face! No wrinkles. No sags. Firm girl flesh filmed with translucent base make-up. Her lips shone frosty pink. Honey blonde hair curled in disarray past the shoulders of Lorena's Hound's-tooth Prada jacket.

Lorena stared back at Sherry. Her mouth opened, but no words came out. She gripped Sherry's hand and tugged her across the street through the stalled traffic to a plate glass window. The reflection of two beautiful girls shone dimly in the lamplight.

"It's an Avatar image," Sherry said. It was all she could think of. "Lots of John's and Michael's video games had them. It's a hologram of who you are in this world." She touched her hair, which in the mirror fell like black rain past her shoulders. Her fingers caressed its silky length. "An avatar you can feel?" Sherry whispered. "How can they do that?"

"I don't know. But I'm officially weirded out." Lorena's voice shook. "This is exactly what I looked like at twenty. How did the computer know that?"

"Those blue lights in that little room?" Sherry said. "Maybe they were some kind of memory scan." She looked at Lorena uncertainly. "Is it too weird for you? Do you want to go back?"

Lorena hesitated. She shook her head. "No. Whatever it is, it feels wonderful. We came for an adventure. Let's have it." She pointed at the mannequin in the next window. "Look. Costumes. Let's go dress the part."

Sherry approved of the mannequin's orange gold metallic mini-dress with long flowing pirate sleeves. "She looks like Twiggy."

"I want that dress," Lorena said. She walked into the shop.

Sherry stopped inside the doorway, overwhelmed by the smell of incense and the blaring Pink Floyd music. A framed neon poster of Pink Floyd's 1966 concert jostled the Beatles Abbey Road poster and The Stones poster, with its trademark big lips. A black and white Herman's Hermits portrait hung above the counter. Dresses filled circular displays with a jewel-whirl of color. Shoe shelves filled one wall. Pointy shoes, spike heel shoes, platform shoes, shoes with ties, shoes with flirty bows, metallic red, rainbow, neon, and vinyl boots. Joy bubbled through her. She was in vintage heaven.

The sales girl wore a skintight black jersey with an almost invisible black miniskirt. Long false eyelashes and kohl liner gave her eyes a sultry look worthy of Elizabeth Taylor. Lorena peered at her nametag. "Hi, Jane. Do you take American Express?"

Jane smiled. "Americans, are you? We call them Traveler's Cheques. And yes, we do."

"Excellent." Lorena rifled through the racks until she found the dress from the window. She selected a pair of gold stack heels with outrageous buckles. "I'll try these on." She disappeared into the red woven curtains at the back of the store.

Sherry prowled the dress racks. This was better than her store because it was all new. She fondled a red silk-tiered mini, then moved on to a mint green mini overlaid in feathers. She sneezed. No feathers, she decided regretfully. Selecting a long sleeved green maxi with a demure lace collar, she held it up to herself in the mirror. She couldn't stop smiling. How wonderful to look as young as she felt.

Lorena came out wearing the dress and shoes. "I'll take these," she announced.

Jane joined Sherry at the mirror. "That dress will look a treat on you. The green matches your eyes. Would you like to try it on?"

Sherry nodded, and headed to the changing room.

Lorena fumbled in her purse for the travelers' checks. "How much?"

"That will be twenty-five pounds, ten."

Lorena took Sherry's place at the mirror. She grinned at her reflection. "Fabulous!"

Sherry came out of the dressing room wearing the maxi dress and carrying their clothes.

"I'll pay for hers too." She took the clothes from Sherry. "Twenty-five pounds, ten. What's that in American?" she whispered.

"In 1969 it was about eighty-five dollars."

Lorena's mouth dropped open. "Seriously? This is cheaper than Nordstrom's Rack." She scanned the shop and grabbed a fringed wool shawl which complimented her dress. "I'll have this as well."

Jane totted up their purchases. She wrapped their old clothes in silver tissue and popped them into a bag that said *Kate's on Carnaby.*

"This is supposed to be Carnaby Street?"

Jane looked uncomfortable. "Oh, well. It's not *really* Carnaby Street. I mean, that's two blocks up. But it sounds posh, don nit?"

Sherry stood in front of the mirror still processing their altered appearances.

Jane accepted two travelers' checks and counted out the change. "You both look spiffy. Got dates for tonight?"

Lorena turned over the unfamiliar money. "I can't remember what a date feels like."

Sherry nodded a rueful agreement.

"Right now food would be wonderful." Lorena turned to Jane. "Where do you recommend?"

"Depends on what you are in the mood for," Jane replied. "Shakespeare's does a smashing bacon and egg pie and the ale's good. Of course if you are feeling flush, there is Cromaniere's." She bowed her head reverently. "It's French."

"Shakespeare's it is," Lorena said. "I always wanted to visit a real English pub."

They said goodbye and stepped back on the street. A chill wind had sprung up.

Sherry shivered. "Weird. My body feels as young as my face looks. No twinges."

Lorena nodded. "Yeah. Feels like I had a body transplant."

"The boys used to be scared of Pirates of the Caribbean at Disneyland when they were young. They said it was too real. Now I know how they felt."

Lorena reached up and stroked her firm smooth cheek. "If I didn't know this was a game, I'd think we time traveled."

"Huh?"

"Never mind. Let's eat."

Chapter 3

The pub's few small round tables were all occupied and the room buzzed with conversations broken by the thump of darts and an occasional crack of laughter.

Sherry breathed in the warm smoky air laced with the scent of bangers and bacon and egg pies. "Oh yes. I remember this." She maneuvered through the small crowd surrounding the darts players and found an empty space at the tall mahogany bar.

The barkeeper caught sight of Sherry and snapped to attention. "What'll it be, luv? And what are you doing after closing? I get off in an hour."

He had to be all of twenty-five and he was flirting with her? She couldn't remember the last time a man gave her that kind of look. This was fun. "I'm a bit old for you, but thanks for the compliment. I'll have two of everything you've got and a couple of ginger beers."

He slapped two plates on the table. He put a bacon and egg pie and a scotch egg on each. "Steak and kidney too?" he asked.

"Absolutely." Sherry fluttered her eyelashes.

Lorena rolled her eyes.

"Where are the bangers?" Sherry sniffed the air. "I know I smell them."

He pointed toward the kitchen. "They'll come separate. You want beans with those?"

"Absolutely!"

He pushed the plates toward them. "American, are you?"

"Yeah." Lorena looked suspiciously at the cold pie. She took a small bite. Her eyes widened. "Not bad, but that may be my hunger talking."

Sherry grabbed the other plate and the ginger beers and angled toward the only unoccupied bench.

Lorena started to follow. "That'll be one pound, six and ten," the barkeep said.

Lorena turned back and got out her wallet. She chose the largest of the bills Jane had given her in change. "I'm not up on your money. Will this cover it?"

"That'll do it." He took the bill and gave her back three smaller ones and some coins. "Here you go."

Lorena picked up her plate and followed Sherry. "I need a lesson in British currency. It all looks like play money to me."

"I take back everything I thought about VR games. This is wonderful." Sherry gestured toward the empty chair. "Sit. Eat. Drink." She took a sip of the ginger beer and hummed rapturously.

Lorena took a sip of her drink and almost spat it out. "What is this stuff? It's disgusting!"

"Ginger beer."

Lorena curled her lip. "Those two words should not be in the same sentence, much less in the same glass."

"I didn't drink when I lived here," Sherry defended, "not alcohol anyway. Couldn't afford it and didn't like it much."

Lorena shoved her ginger beer toward Sherry. "I am so not drinking that. Do you suppose they have any wine?"

"Don't know. You could try the porter. I'm told it's good."

"Porter? As in person who carries your bags?"

Sherry snorted. "No! Porter as in dark brown ale."

Lorena walked back to the bar. "What's your name?" she asked the barkeep.

"Andrew," he shouted over the sudden burst of cheering from the corner darts game.

"Well, Andrew, my friend said I should try the porter. Can you give me a little taste?" Lorena fluttered her own lashes. No response. Was she losing it?

Andrew built a pint and offered it to her.

"Hmmm." She licked her lips clear of foam. "Not bad. I'll take one."

Lorena wove her way back to Sherry and sat down gracefully. "The porter's rather good. I feel very British." She took a sip of porter, reached into her purse, and pulled out a pack of cigarettes.

"I thought you'd given up smoking."

"That was yesterday. I've changed my mind." Lorena lit up—inhaled–and started coughing. "Yech." She stubbed it out. "That's weird. It tastes terrible. I guess this body is younger than twenty-seven. That's when I started smoking."

Sherry grinned. "Now that's just excellent."

"Bangers up," Andrew called.

Sherry went to retrieve them.

Lorena stood up and peered out the window, tapping her fingers on the pane. The blue veins in her hands were gone. The whole damn thing felt so real. Wait . . . She returned to the table. "Aha! The game designers slipped up." She waved at the lamp lit night. "No fog. Remember that song, *Foggy Day in London Town* . . .? They got it wrong!"

Sherry disagreed. "No, they got it right. When I first got to London, I thought there was something missing, but I couldn't think what it was. Then I remembered the foggy day song. I asked my flatmate. She said they banished the smog in the late fifties with something called the *Clean Air Act*."

"That sucks. I wanted to see the fog. All the books and movies I read talk about it."

"Oscar Wilde said there was no fog in London until the artist William Turner began painting it. After Turner, novelists began to write about fog in London." Sherry drained her ginger beer and reached for Lorena's. "There was no fog in London in Shakespeare or Ben Johnson's writings, but there was a lot of it in Dickens's and Doyle's stories and . . ."

Lorena put her finger to Sherry's lips. "You're chatting inanely. You know that, right?"

Sherry nodded. "Inane chat helps me deal with the sense of bizarreness I'm feeling."

"Makes sense." Lorena downed half her glass of porter. "So where's the swinging part of London?"

"I don't have a clue."

"But you lived here. You must have some idea."

"Lorena, in 1969 my idea of swinging was browsing the shops in Bond Street and an occasional trip to the Royal Ballet." What had she been so afraid of? Sherry smiled ruefully. "The one chance I had at adventure sent me running in the opposite direction."

"Last call, Ladies and Gents."

There was a rush to the bar.

"Keep the table," Sherry said. "I'll get us a last round."

She joined the throng at the bar stepping back a bit to keep some air space between her and the fragrant man in front of her who obviously didn't believe in deodorant. She stepped on a foot and turned around to apologize.

Hands rested on her shoulders steadying her. "Sorry about that, luv. I'm being pressed from behind."

She looked up into sea blue eyes warm with amusement. Her pulse kicked up. He could have posed for an ad in Vogue. Six foot two with chestnut hair curling down to the collar of his gray three piece suit. She inhaled the orangey, clove odor of his aftershave. There was something about him. Her mouth dropped open as a memory bloomed from a long ago hot August day in London . . .

Sherry glanced around with a frown. Why did the tube have to be crowded? Not an empty strap to be had. She stood in the center of the car concentrating on keeping her balance, her arms slightly out, thoughts turned inward, gaze unfocussed to protect her privacy.

A sudden lurch of the train threw her up against another freestanding passenger. She looked up at him to murmur an automatic apology. His equally automatic response was interrupted by the opening of the tube door . . .

The man looked down at her with a puzzled flicker of recognition "I know you . . ."

She could only stare at him and remember . . .

Twenty or thirty more people pushed into the car. They were all shoved together like trash in a compacter. Her distaste for this invasion of personal space was mirrored in the incredibly handsome face of the stranger now pressed against her. He glanced down at her. His sea blue eyes widened and he smiled.

Sherry's irritation vanished. She grinned back.

They both melted into laughter. The laughter stopped and became something else. Tightly pressed together, their eyes quested for and found . . . He bent down. She reached up. They exchanged a gentle soft recognizing kiss.

"What's your name?" he asked, bringing her back to the present.

"Sherry," she said, in a trance. "Sherry Southerland and you're . . ."

"Jeremy." He touched her cheek lightly with the back of his fingers. "Jeremy Smythe."

Jeremy Smythe. The name echoed in her mind. They hadn't known each other, but for that one brief moment, they'd been one.

At the next stop, the train emptied out. Stepping back, they resumed their own spaces.

Can I see you again?" he asked.

What had she done? "No. This was perfect. Let's leave it that way."

He smiled and agreed. Had there been a shadow in his eyes?

They exchanged one more soft kiss and Sherry left the train. They'd made a magical moment she'd never forgotten and always regretted. Why hadn't she said yes?

Jeremy's eyes lit up. "You're the girl on the tube. We met . . ." he paused, "almost three months ago. August, wasn't it?"

Sherry nodded wordlessly. August. 1969. Her brain spun in dizzying circles. How could this man from her past be in a VR game? It wasn't possible.

Jeremy smoothed away the frown she hadn't been aware of wearing. "Looks like we've intersected again."

Maybe this really is 1969, she thought wildly. *Should I believe in second chances?*

"When you eliminate the impossible, whatever remains, however improbable must be the truth," she said aloud.

"Aha, a fellow Sherlock Holmes fan, I see."

The bar crowd pressed them up against each other.

"History repeats itself." Jeremy bent down and brought his lips to hers. Sweetly, gently. It was like coming home.

Sherry felt a sharp pinch on her arm. "Ow!" She broke away from Jeremy and turned to find the pincher.

"Excuse me." Lorena stood there tapping her foot. She didn't look happy.

Jeremy reached for Sherry's hand. She could feel the warmth of his clasp tingling up her arm. "Lorena, this is Jeremy. He's, uh . . . an old friend."

Lorena eyed Jeremy suspiciously. "Good friend by the looks of it."

"Jeremy and I met by chance in . . ."

"August. On the tube." Jeremy smiled. "We became close."

Sherry giggled.

"Excuse us for a minute." Lorena pulled Sherry aside. "You shouldn't be too friendly with the actors in the game. Believe me, you don't want to date an actor."

"I don't think he's an actor," Sherry whispered. "I met Jeremy in 1969. I know it's not possible. But this is Jeremy. I never forgot that meeting."

Lorena froze. "Are you saying this is really 1969?"

Sherry nodded. "Think about it. That weird dizzy feeling in the room. Our changed bodies. She took a deep breath and quoted. 'When you eliminate the impossible . . .'"

"Whatever remains, however improbably must be the truth," finished Lorena. "*Casebook of Sherlock Holmes.*" She gripped Sherry's arm. "Okay. Time to go home."

Sherry resisted. "Not yet." The same magic she'd felt that day on the train shimmered in the air. "Lorena, I need to follow this. I know it."

Lorena looked unnerved. "If this is time travel, we don't know the rules. All I remember from my reading is you can't stay and you shouldn't change anything. I think we'd better leave."

"I'm not talking about staying a long time. I know that would change things . . ."

"Yeah," Lorena interrupted, "like the existence of our children. You have to meet Bill and I have to meet Dave."

"But we could stay for a while. A week maybe?"

"No."

"Think of the history," Sherry wheedled. "Think of the shopping."

Jeremy joined them. "Are you visiting from America this time? Where are you staying?"

Sherry looked at Lorena pleadingly.

Lorena shrugged in defeat. "Our luggage got lost and we haven't picked a hotel yet," she improvised. "Can you recommend a good one?"

If Jeremy thought that was odd, he concealed it well. "The Cadogan is good. It's on Sloane Street in Knightsbridge. It's got nice rooms and it's rather historical. Do you like that kind of thing? Lily Langtry, the actress, used to live there."

Lorena looked intrigued. "I liked Lily Langtry. I mean I didn't know her personally, but I like her style."

"Can I drive you there? I've got my car."

"Yes, please," Sherry said. She turned and whispered to Lorena, "If you don't have a passport, we may be in trouble."

"Since The Homeland Security Act, I always carry it," Lorena replied. "It makes life a lot easier."

"Excellent," Sherry said. "Now as long as they don't check the date . . ."

Lorena took a deep breath. "Here goes nothing."

Chapter 4

Jeremy ushered them to a silver 1965 Aston Martin. Lorena's mouth dropped open. "Holy cow, it's the James Bond car. I love it!"

"It's my car, actually," Jeremy said with a straight face. "I loan it to James for special occasions." He opened the door for them.

"Oh, right." Lorena sniffed. "Make fun of the American." She squirmed her way into the back seat.

Sherry inhaled the rich scent of leather. As Jeremy helped her into the front seat, the warmth of his hand burned through her dress. She shivered.

"What's this homeland security act I heard you mention?" Jeremy expertly navigated through the press of traffic. "Something to do with Vietnam?"

Sherry couldn't think of anything to say that wouldn't sound crazy. She kept silent.

Lorena broke in, "So Jeremy, what do you do for a living?"

"I run a small magazine called *Twenty-Eight*."

Lorena leaned forward. "What type of articles do you print?"

Jeremy glanced over his shoulder at her. "I run the kind of magazine where if someone calls me up and says their goldfish is talking to them, I don't talk about hot baths and soothing drinks. I say, 'Put the goldfish on the phone'."

Lorena snorted. "You're kidding. Right?"

"I would never make sport of a goldfish," Jeremy said

gravely. He stopped in front of The Cadogan, got out and opened the doors for Sherry and Lorena.

Lorena squared her shoulders and walked toward the pillared entryway.

Jeremy pulled Sherry around to face him. "Listen, I thought you might like a walk or something. We still haven't talked." He brushed a stray hair off her cheek. "Don't run away this time," he whispered.

Sherry caught her breath. "Yes. Wait for me. I won't be long."

Potted palms changed groups of chairs into oases. Lorena paused to study the two oil paintings glowing on the walnut paneled walls of the reception area. "That's Lily Langtry," she whispered to Sherry. "And I think the other one is her lover, Edward Prince of Wales. He's wearing Royal Orders. I already love this place."

They walked up to the mahogany grill. The man behind it had no nametag. His suit and bearing said he was an important person. He smiled an austere welcome. "Good evening. May I look up your reservation?"

"We don't have one," Lorena replied. She pulled out her travelers checks and handed them to him. "We'd like a double suite please."

His expression brightened as he flipped through the sheaf. "Of course, madam. The Langtry Suite is available." He pulled off four checks and presented them for her signature. "I'll have your bags sent up." He looked for their non-existent luggage and frowned. "If I might see your identification?"

"The airline lost our bags," Lorena explained. She flipped open her passport so he couldn't see the cover. "We will be shopping in the morning."

The maroon uniformed elevator operator pulled the lever to close the door. The elevator moved upward with the ponderous grace of an old dowager. "Not very busy this time of night," he said. "I'll see you to your room."

He unlocked the carved rosewood door.

"Wow. I feel like I've walked onto the set of a Noel Coward play." Lorena took in the embossed silver leaf wallpaper and heavy jade drapes. She arranged herself à la film star on the aqua damask sofa. "I need a slipper satin evening dress and a cigarette holder to fit in."

A Queen Anne table held a bowl of fresh fruit, four Waterford goblets, and a crystal decanter filled with amber liquid. "What's in the decanter?" Lorena asked.

"Brandy, Madam." He bowed. "If you need anything at all, ring the front desk. The door closed behind him with a soft *snick*.

Lorena kicked off her shoes and curled her legs under her. "You know, I always thought that heaven was a really good hotel."

"Let's see the bedroom and then I'm going out. I have to talk to Jeremy."

The bedroom was sumptuous. Peach silk draperies over arched windows. A jade brocade bedspread covered the four-poster bed. Lorena fingered the ivory satin puff folded at the foot of the chaise lounge. "I'd like to take this home with me."

The rococo table beside the chaise held an old-fashioned radio, a reading lamp, and a pile of magazines. Sherry picked up the Vogue magazine that topped the pile. The cover picture was titled, *Englishwoman 1969,* and featured a wide-eyed beauty wearing a tall fur hat.

Lorena opened the tall white Louis XIV style wardrobe that dominated one wall. It held a twenty-inch Zenith television. The television had a dial to change channels. There was no remote. "Dare I hope it's color?"

"I didn't have color TV in 1969. I think it existed though."

The fitted drawer of the bedside table revealed an elaborate maroon and gold booklet with an extensive room service menu.

"Excellent. Go meet your Jeremy." Lorena sprawled in the middle of the bed. "I'm going to draw a bath and find some music on the radio and call room service."

"Are you sure you don't mind?"

Lorena clasped her hands behind her head. "I've decided to enjoy the moment. Although I'm still not sure this is real. Maybe Mr. Chow's served us spiked dumplings and tomorrow we'll wake up in our own beds."

"I hope not." Sherry couldn't think past Jeremy's kiss. One thing she knew for certain. This time she didn't want to run.

Chapter 5

Jeremy looked at ease lounging against the Aston Martin. Sherry's nerves hummed. Her mind was still processing the fact that they'd gone back in time and the man she'd never stopped dreaming about was there in front of her. *Breathe,* she reminded herself. She took a calming breath and exhaled. Her breath floated out in a cloud of vapor.

"Not the best night for a walk." Jeremy took off his suit jacket and fitted it around her shoulders. His hands lingered, thumbs stroking a trail of heat down her neck.

Sherry fingered the fine weave of the jacket. Who knew the scent of warm wool could be an aphrodisiac. Well that and the faint tangy aroma of Jeremy's aftershave. Her pulse quickened.

"Pity the pubs are all closed." He tucked her hand through his arm as they turned onto Sloan Street.

Sherry tried to think of something witty to say, but her brain was stuck on stupid.

Jeremy broke the silence. "I'm trying to think of something clever to say, but my mind's gone to Bristol." The warm, amused look in his eyes, invited her to share the joke.

"If I knew where Bristol was, I'd say my mind was there playing with yours." She dropped her eyes. *Oh no, did that sound like a come on?*

They turned into a park. The mellow glow from the globed streetlights cast their shadows before them. The dew damp shrubbery added to the chill in the air.

"This used to be the London Botanic Gardens a long

time ago. It's beautiful in the daylight and—" He scowled. "You're shivering. This is daft."

Jeremy enfolded her icy hands in his warm grasp. "Let me take you to my flat."

"Said the spider to the fly." Sherry tensed her jaw to keep her teeth from chattering.

"This isn't a come-on. I promise." He turned their steps back to the hotel. "I make a mean cup of tea. I'll light up the gas fireplace and we'll have a warm chat." He halted and looked down at her. "That didn't come out quite right, did it? I meant we'll chat and our bodies will warm up."

Sherry laughed at the look on his face.

Jeremy's lips curved. "You'd never think I read English at Oxford, would you? I'm usually quite well spoken, but when I look at you, my brain feels like it's . . ."

"Somewhere else?" she offered. Sherry had a pretty good idea of where his brain had gone. Hers was drifting in that direction too.

"Oh, hell." He dropped his forehead to hers. "I'll be very circumspect," he whispered.

I'm not sure how circumspect I want you to be. She resisted the temptation to run her fingers over the angled planes of his face.

"Come with me, Sherry. I want to show you where I live."

Sherry nodded and slipped into the car. She reached for the nonexistent seat belt, then hastily folded her hands in her lap, hoping Jeremy hadn't noticed. "You've no idea how strange this feels."

"That it is." Jeremy engaged the car and zipped out into the busy lane. "What are the odds of the two people being pressed together twice in a city the size of London? I think it's the Octopus of Fate."

Sherry turned to him in incredulous delight. "You read Phoebe Atwood Taylor? I adore Leonidas Witherall."

"How could you not love a man who looks like Shakespeare's identical twin and carries a Lady Baltimore cake for the length of an entire novel?" Jeremy pulled to a stop in front of a Georgian townhouse.

"Well," Sherry drew a quick breath, willing herself to appear calm. "You live very close to the Cadogan."

"That's why I recommended it," Jeremy admitted. "I wanted you nearby." He came round the car, opened the passenger door, and offered his hand to her. Sherry took it, letting the heat of his palm envelop hers. The evening air had begun to mist, giving a cloudy dreamlike look to the light from the lantern fixture by the door. Unlocking the front door of the townhouse, he ushered her inside.

Sherry glanced around curiously, her body relaxing in the interior warmth. Electric candle sconces flanked the two doors on either side of the hallway. A red stair runner in a Turkish design climbed the mahogany dark steps to a second floor. Jeremy led her into the sitting room and switched on the lights.

She clapped her hands. "I love it!" Was that her voice? Ick. She sounded like a teenager.

Fat Wedgewood lamps cast golden shadows on the dark wood paneling. A television in a walnut cabinet sat to the left of a gas fireplace. Shelves to the right of the fireplace contained a stereo system and a huge selection of LPs.

She opened her mouth to comment on him having kept his record collection when she remembered when she was. Was she going to give herself away? Probably. She focused on the oil painting above the fireplace. A fragile clipper ship cresting impossibly blue waves.

"That ship reminds me of Keats."

Jeremy nodded. "Magic casements, opening on the foam of perilous seas in fairy lands forlorn.'" That's why I bought it."

He knew Keats. She'd always dreamed of a man who could quote poetry. Everything about Jeremy drew her in. Why hadn't she said yes that day in the tube? But then, John and Michael wouldn't exist. Everything comes with a price.

"What's wrong?" Jeremy's eyes filled with concern. "You look like you're carrying the weight of the world on your shoulders."

How about the weight of sixty-three years?

"If you want to talk about it, I'm a good listener. Maybe I could help."

How to begin? How about *I'm a little freaked out because I'm a time traveler and I've no idea how to tell you that?*

"Nothing's wrong." Avoiding his eyes, she crossed over to the floor to ceiling bookshelves lining the right hand wall. Sherry caressed the smooth book spines. "You have all my favorites. Tolkien, C.S. Lewis." She moved on, running her fingers along the mystery titles. "Christie, Allingham, Tey, Rex Stout, and here's Leonidas Witherall." She smiled at him. "I'm glad you read Americans as well as the English writers."

"I see we are fellow bookaholics." Jeremy quirked an eyebrow. "I'll brew us a pot of tea and we can have a meeting."

"Bookaholics? I like that." She fought the urge to reach up and smooth his eyebrows and followed him through the dining room into the kitchen.

Jeremy crossed to the double sink, filled the teapot, and lit the red Aga.

Sherry willed herself to concentrate on the ambience rather than Jeremy. She liked how the red of the stove repeated in the knobs of the white enameled cupboards, and the diamond shaped insets in the black tile floor.

The matching tile countertop held a row of china canisters made like whimsical animals.

"Where did you get those amazing canisters?"

Jeremy reddened. "An old girlfriend." He reached into the dancing elephant and brought out a box of Cadbury's Chocolate fingers. "She was into pottery. She made them."

Sherry leaned against the counter, enjoying his look of embarrassment. "What happened? Why aren't you together anymore?"

"She moved out in September. Said I was getting boring. She said I was a bit distracted."

"Were you?"

He gave a half nod, arranging the biscuits on a white stoneware plate. "Well, the magazine was going through a rough patch, and there was this girl I met on the tube . . ."

"I broke you up?" Sherry asked disbelieving.

Jeremy laughed. "Well the memory of you might have, but the truth is there was this guitar player she fancied. He looked a lot like Paul McCartney. She moved in with him." He proffered the plate. "Biscuit?"

She bit into one of the fingers, savoring the smooth rich chocolate. "I might have been tempted by Paul McCartney."

Jeremy brought her hand to his mouth and took a bite of her chocolate. "If I was Paul McCartney, would you have given me your number?"

"Maybe." Sherry caught her breath. She wanted to taste him.

He raised one eyebrow.

"Okay. Probably."

Jeremy turned to the panda canister and spooned tea into a plain brown pot.

"I would have known who Paul McCartney was," Sherry defended. "You were simply this incredibly good looking man who kissed like . . ." She felt her body grow warm. "You could have been Jack the Ripper for all I knew."

"I could see it felt a bit daft to you, kissing a total stranger. But you didn't feel like a stranger to me." Jeremy hesitated. He smiled crookedly. "It sounds stupid when I put it into words. You felt more like a friend I had been waiting to find." He leaned against the counter and crossed his arms. "I tried to find your name on the exchange. I thought perhaps I didn't spell it properly."

"I didn't have a phone. I was staying at Hyde House YWCA." She was mesmerized by a tiny crumb of chocolate at the corner of his mouth.

"Pity. I was going to find someone to introduce us properly. I had my godmother in mind. She reeks of respectability." He picked up a teaspoon and used it as a lorgnette. "Miss Southerland, this is my godson, Jeremy," he said in a falsetto voice, pruning his mouth like an old lady's. "He's the editor of an up and coming magazine called *Twenty-Eight* and has no incurable bad habits. May I present him to you as an eligible suitor?"

Sherry stifled a bubble of laughter. "Someone's been reading Georgette Heyer."

"My sister reads her all the time. I may have picked up one she left lying around." He bowed gravely and reached for her hand. "I'm delighted to make your acquaintance, Miss Southerland."

Sherry curtsied demurely. "Enchanted, Mr. Smythe." She reached up and brushed away the crumb from his mouth.

Jeremy caught her hand and sucked her finger.

Sherry felt a tingle which started in her toes and trickled up to her brain. He's the one. This is what I've been waiting for.

With a gentle tug, he clasped his hands behind her back.

Sherry lifted her face to meet his gaze. His kiss was soft. Slow at first . . .

Sherry freed her hands and wove her fingers through his crisp chestnut curls, drawing him closer. The delicate ridges clung and wrapped around her fingertips. The kiss deepened into a dance of tongues. All thoughts slipped from her mind.

There was nothing but feeling. Their bodies molded together, missing pieces of a puzzle long separated, and melted to the floor.

The whistle of the teakettle sounded sharp and piercing.

A voice from the doorway interrupted them. "Ooh, tea. Exactly what I wanted."

Chapter 6

A young woman wearing a faux fur jacket lounged in the doorway. "Don't let me stop you, darling. I like a good show."

Sherry broke free of the kiss and sat up willing her heartbeat toward normality.

"Shut up, Jen." Jeremy rose in a lithe easy movement and pulled Sherry to her feet. He frowned at the beautiful redhead. "For an actress you have a lousy sense of timing."

He had a girlfriend. Sherry froze, feeling naked in her clothes. What a fool I am. "I thought you said you weren't with anyone."

"I'm not. This is my dill of a sister, Jennifer." Jeremy pulled Sherry to him in a protective embrace. "What are you doing here, Jen?"

Jen flicked away a non-existent piece of lint from her collar. "Kerry put out the red scarf. So I thought I'd bunk with you tonight. Sorry to interrupt such a tender moment. I didn't know you had a bird." Jen poured the boiling water into the teapot and reached into the cupboard for three cups. "Shall I play mother?"

Sherry felt Jeremy's body stiffen.

"Of all the . . ." Jeremy glared at Jen. "Red scarf? What are you playing at?"

"It's our signal. In case one of us has a friend for the night."

Jeremy straightened his shoulders and frowned down at his sister. "I'd better not find out you've used the red scarf. I'll pack you straight home to Mum and Dad."

"Ooh, look!" Jen fluttered her hands at Jeremy. "The Pot calling the Kettle."

"I'm three years older than you. It's a very different thing."

Sherry giggled. "Peace, you two. You sound like my s—" Sherry bit off the word *sons*. "My sister and I." She smiled at Jen. "Hi. I'm Sherry. And your brother and I won't be putting out the red scarf." Jeremy's hand tightened around her waist. "At least not tonight," she amended.

"You're American. Where in America?" Jen looked at Sherry's green wool maxi with a disparaging eye. She reached for the rooster shaped creamer. "Milk?"

"Los Angeles. And yes to the milk."

Jen's eyes lit up. "Los Angeles! Do you know any movie stars?" She poured milk in the cups and added the tea. "I'd love to meet Jon Voight and Dustin Hoffman. They're fabulous actors. *Midnight Cowboy* was supreme."

What could she say? How about she'd never met Jon, but his daughter, Angelina, came into her shop regularly? Sherry shook her head.

"You're not an actress?" Jen handed her a cup of tea and pushed the frog canister toward her. "Sugar?"

Sherry picked up the frog and decided to change the subject. "I could sell these canisters in a minute at *Now and Then*."

"And what's *Now and Then*?" Jen asked.

"My store. I sell vintage clothes and furniture and . . ." Sherry caught herself. The canisters weren't vintage in 1969. Think! "And, uh, anything else that catches my fancy. It doesn't have to be vintage. I sell lots of modern jewelry and pottery. That's the *Now* part of *Now and Then*. I like the unusual."

"That's another thing we have in common." Jeremy reached for her hand. "I'll give them to you. I'll even call Jessica and ask if she'll make you another set."

Jen reached over and took the frog from Sherry. "So where'd you meet Jeremy?" She asked, adding a heaping teaspoon of sugar to her tea. The honey in her voice clashed with the spark of mischief in her eyes.

Jeremy caught the look and his gaze promised retribution. "Jen, why don't you take your cup of tea and toddle off? I'm sure you're ready to climb into bed with a good book. Or better still, go back to your flat and interrupt Kerry."

Jen assumed a pious expression. "I'm making lovely conversation. The two of you smell too much of April and May. I don't want you two doing anything you'll regret."

"April and May?" Jeremy looked befuddled.

"Georgette Heyer," Sherry mouthed to him and sighed inwardly. Jen wasn't going to stop. She was having too much fun irritating her brother. The Octopus of Fate was not on their side in this one.

Jeremy looked at Jen and muttered something under his breath. He led the way back to the living room and set a match to the gas fireplace. Tongues of blue and gold flames cast shadows on the walls. He pulled Sherry down next to him on the sofa. "I'd put on a record, but under the circumstances, it's probably inappropriate."

"I'll pick a record," Jen said. "Got any Leonard Cohen? *Suzanne* would fit the bill. She sang, *"And you want to travel with her and you want to travel blind . . ."*

"I should have smothered her as a baby," Jeremy remarked to the air. "Sit down, Jen, and try to pretend you're civilized."

Jen perched on the armchair and beamed at them. "So, what has Jeremy told you about us?"

Jeremy looked at Jen as if she'd grown a second head. "Why would I tell her anything about you at all?"

"Jennifer feels we should know a lot about each other," Sherry interposed. "She's looking out for you." She beamed right back at Jen. "Tell me about yourself, Jeremy. Start with where you were born and work up gradually."

"Kent. It's one of the Home Counties. It borders London. It's beautiful, lots of gardens and orchards." He reached behind her and caught a lock of her hair, winding it around his fingers. "This feels like the kind of thing one says on a first date."

"Or the kind of thing one says in front of a little sister." She gave Jen an angelic smile. "I was born in Redbank, New Jersey. I was an adorable child who loved to play paper dolls and cowboys and Indians. Occasionally I scalped my dolls, but I was always sorry afterward. What did you like to do?"

"Soul mates. I knew it." Jeremy grinned. "I loved cowboys and Indians. And I scalped the occasional doll, when my sisters left one unguarded."

Jen nodded. "He was a trial, but Rob was the worst. He . . ." Her eyes shadowed and welled up. A tear tracked a path of mascara down her face. "Excuse me, please." Shoulders stiff, she hurried out of the room.

Sherry saw the same shadow in Jeremy's eyes. She reached for his hand. "Who's Rob?"

"Robert. My older brother."

"What happened to him?"

"Insurgents captured the peace mission he headed in Rhodesia last year. They shot Rob to make a statement."

Sherry gripped his hand tightly. "I'm so sorry. I can't imagine what it's like to lose a brother."

"Yeah." Jeremy stared at the fire. His face showed no emotion. "It was harder on my parents. Rob was their first-born. The dreamer. He was going to change the world."

The thought of losing John or Michael was like a knife in her heart. "There ought to be a law that children can't die before their parents."

Jeremy's lips curved in a ghost of a smile. "I'm sure parents everywhere would appreciate it." He pulled Sherry into his arms. "Now that we're finally alone . . ." He cradled the back of her head in his hand and took possession of her lips.

Where had he learned to kiss like that? Sherry put her hands on his shoulder and drew him closer.

"Sorry about that. I must have gotten something in my eye." Jen plopped back down on the chair, smiling brightly. "So where were we?"

Jeremy broke the kiss and scowled at Jen. "Leaving." He rose and held out his hand to Sherry. "I'm taking Sherry back to her hotel."

She stood, grateful for his support. Kissing him played havoc with her equilibrium. "It was nice meeting you, Jen. I hope I'll see you again before I leave."

"Oh, you're here on a visit then?"

"Yes my friend, Lorena, and I got in today. We lost our luggage, so tomorrow we'll be shopping."

Jen clapped her hands. "Shopping is my favorite sport." Her face fell. "If I didn't have rehearsal I'd join you. I know some lovely shops. There's Biba on Regent Street and . . ." She quailed at the look in Jeremy's eyes.

"Go to bed, Jen. If I see you when I get home, I might do something drastic."

The ride back to the hotel was silent. Jeremy drove well with one hand. The other fondled Sherry's fingers, sending little spurts of electricity through her body and bringing her unfulfilled desire to the boiling point. He pulled to a stop in front of the Cadogan and sighed. "It's probably for the good. I don't seem to have any control where you're concerned."

Sherry drew his head down to hers. "Feeling's mutual," she whispered. This time her lips did the capturing. Time stopped. A sharp impatient honk sounded.

Jeremy broke the kiss with a groan. "I give up." He opened the door and went round to help her out of the car. "Meet me in the lobby tomorrow at one. I'll take you and your friend to lunch." He took a slim case out of his vest pocket and handed her a card. "This has both my numbers in case you need to reach me before that."

Sherry rubbed her fingers over the raised silver letters. "Very elegant. I'm impressed."

"Excellent. My new goal in life is to impress you."

When he wrapped his arms around her, she could feel the evidence of his frustration.

He stepped back and kissed her lightly on her nose. "Don't run away again, Sherry," he whispered. "Please stay."

She nodded wordlessly and walked into the lobby.

Chapter 7

"Jeremy?" Sherry scrunched her eyes shut to avoid a stabbing shaft of sunlight. She sat up and looked at her bed companion.

Lorena. Dead to the world, her breath puffing her hair off her face.

"Rats."

She flopped back and pillowed her face in her hands. *Jeremy.* Every time he touched her last night, all she'd wanted to do was fuse her body to his so that nothing could come between them.

Last night she'd promised she wouldn't run away again. Stupid, Stupid, Stupid! What was she thinking? She knew she couldn't stay, but . . . Had she ever felt like this with Bill? No. Not like this. She closed her eyes and savored the memory of last night. To be held with love after so many years of not being touched. To know someone was waiting. That someone wanted her as much as she wanted him.

Sherry winced. Yeah, but how would he feel when he found out how old she was? She couldn't tell him. Not yet. Whatever they made together in this little space in time would have to last her for the rest of her life.

Sherry rolled over and stared at plaster lover's knots bordering the ceiling. How was she going to convince Lorena to stay?

Soothe her with food.

She reached into the bedside table drawer and pulled out a menu.

Belting the hotel robe around her she hurried to the living room and picked up the phone. "Room service, please." She smiled down at the old-fashioned phone. Everything made her think of smiling. She had a feeling that if a policeman wanted to arrest her right now, she'd smile and say, "*It's a lovely day for that.*"

A voice crackled on the other end of the phone. "Good morning, Room service. May I take your order?"

"Good morning. This is room three hundred and twelve. Could you please send up two full English breakfasts, and a large pot of tea?"

"Twenty minutes. Will that be satisfactory?"

"Yes. Thank you." She hung up and twirled around the room. What was that line of Scrooge's from Christmas Carol? Oh yes, *I'm as giddy as a schoolboy.* That described it perfectly.

Time enough for a shower before she tried to wake Lorena. Waking Lorena was like trying to wake a grizzly in the middle of winter. She picked up her crumpled green maxi dress. Shopping was definitely in order.

"Lorena, wake up!"

Nothing. Sherry leaned over and shook her. Drops of water flew from Sherry's wet hair and landed on Lorena's face.

Lorena pulled the covers over her head. "Not now, Dylan. Grandma's sleeping."

Sherry pulled the covers back. "Wake up. Look around."

Lorena opened one eye. "Where's the fire?" she mumbled in a sleep slurred voice. Her one-eyed gaze landed on Sherry. Both eyes popped wide opened. "Who are you?" She propped herself up on one elbow and caught sight of her own honey blonde hair tangled around her. "Okaaay. It's coming back now. We went to this new place, The Castle, for a VR game. It made you feel like you were in England in 1969." There was a long pause. "Where am I?"

Sherry sighed. "I ordered breakfast. The tea will wake you up."

"I don't drink tea." Lorena yawned loudly. "I want coffee."

"Believe me on this one. Their coffee is terrible. It doesn't taste like the American stuff."

Sherry heard a knock at the living room door. "Food!"

A maroon liveried bellboy wheeled in a cloth-covered cart and flipped up the sides to make a table. He positioned two high back chairs and busied himself arranging two place settings.

"Lovely," Sherry said, admiring the gold banded Meissen plate and matching teacups. She reached in her purse and found a worn ten-dollar bill. "I'm sorry. I only have American money right now. I hope this will do."

"Cor! That's like three pounds!" His freckled face flamed. "I mean, thank you, Madam. Anything you want, you ask for Jimmy." His whistle carried through the door he shut behind him.

Lorena surveyed the beautifully set table and arrowed in on the teapot. "I hope you're right about the tea waking me up."

"Put the milk in your cup first before you add the tea," Sherry advised. "That's the way they do it over here."

Lorena rolled her eyes, but did as Sherry suggested. She took a sip. Her eyes widened. "Wonderful." She finished the cup and poured another. "This doesn't taste like tea we get in America. It's stronger and better."

"I think it's the water. I bought tea and took it home when I was here before. It didn't taste the same way it did in England." Sherry lifted the silver salvers. Scones, eggs, sausages, and kippers.

"Ugh! What's that awful smell?"

"Kippers." Sherry re-covered them. "I forgot they were part of a traditional British breakfast." She helped herself to sausage and eggs, buttered a scone, and topped it with marmalade from a cut glass dish. "So how was your night?"

"Amazing. That tub is wonderful. I think the bath salts are jasmine. I was going to order room service, but by the time I had a bath and a brandy I was too tired to do anything but sleep." Lorena snagged a scone and buttered it. "So tell me everything. I'm still trying to believe you went out with a total stranger."

"He was not a stranger"

Lorena looked at her skeptically.

"I remembered him." Sherry set down the teacup and curled her legs under her. "Lorena this is the God's honest truth . . ."

"I love stories that start out like that."

Sherry thought about throwing a bit of scone at her, but decided it would be childish. Not to mention messy. "Do you want to hear this or not?"

Lorena leaned back and crossed her legs. "You may proceed."

Sherry sipped her tea and let the rich sharp flavor send her back to 1969. "I met him on the tube. The train was already full when he got in. We were standing fairly close. The door opened and a whole crowd of people got on." Sherry shook her head. "That car made a sardine can seem roomy. I put my face up to breathe and he looked into my eyes. He smiled at me. I smiled back, and . . . It was an irresistible force. We kissed." What a lame word to explain a moment of absolute magic. "And the crazy thing is, it felt completely right."

"Then what happened?"

"He asked if he could call me."

"And?"

"I said no."

Lorena looked at her as if she'd grown a second head. "Why?"

Yeah. Why? Sherry looked into her teacup. "It was this amazing magical moment and I didn't want to spoil it."

"That is so lame," Lorena scoffed.

"Okay, I was scared. I was a kid, alone in a foreign country at a time when Americans weren't too popular. And he was . . . too much. Too beautiful. I couldn't believe that he and I could possibly have anything real together, and I wasn't ready for a one night stand."

"I bet that's a decision you've regretted." Lorena examined her manicure.

"On many occasions," Sherry agreed, thinking of Bill and his flight to a much younger wife. "I never forgot him though. It was a valentine of a memory. And last night when I saw him again, I was ready for the adventure."

"So what happened last night?" Lorena reached for the marmalade. "Titillate me."

"Not much to tell." Sherry savored a bite of sausage. "We're supposed to meet him for lunch today."

"Come on! You're speaking to a woman whose sole experience of physical contact is limited to hugs from my grandson or scripted kissing on the show and you know there's not much of that. Please tell me you at least snogged."

"I think J.K. Rowling made that word up," Sherry said primly. "Or at least they aren't using it right now."

"Your face is getting red. That means there's something to tell. Come on," Lorena cajoled, "did he get to third base? Details will be welcomed."

"Third base?" Sherry raised her eyebrows. "Honestly, Lorena. That one's worse than snogging."

Lorena stared at her expectantly.

"Oh, all right, if you must know. We kissed." Sherry's stomach fluttered in remembrance. "The world exploded and I saw stars. It was as though I'd never been kissed before."

Lorena leaned forward. "And?"

Sherry capitulated. "And if his sister hadn't shown up, we definitely would have made a home run."

"His sister? You're kidding?"

Sherry sighed. "I wish. In the middle of the most fairy tale kiss of my life this gorgeous redhead appears in the doorway. I thought she was his girlfriend."

"How do you know she wasn't?"

"If you heard them argue, you wouldn't have any doubt either. They sounded like John and Michael. Jennifer's an actress. I think you'll like her."

Lorena's eyes lit up. "Now that's something I'd like to see while we're here. I wonder what's playing at the National Theatre. Or the Royal Shakespeare Company. Wouldn't it be marvelous if it was Olivier?"

"Yes." Sherry took a deep breath. "Here's the thing, Lorena. I want to stay."

Chapter 8

Lorena dropped her cup of tea. "But you can't. If this is time travel, you have to go back. You have two kids. If you don't go back, they'll never have been born." She rescued her empty cup

Sherry grabbed a napkin and blotted the dark stain spreading on the carpet. "I know I can't stay forever, but . . ."

"You live in the twenty-first century." Lorena stalked to the breakfast cart and sloshed more tea into her cup, forgetting the milk. "You're sixty-three, for Pete's sake. What happens when he finds out? You've got to tell him."

"I know I do. Just . . . not yet." Sherry leaned forward pleading. "Lorena, we could stay a while. A week. Maybe two."

Lorena eyed her narrowly. "What about our lives in California. Don't you think someone might notice if we're missing?"

"Maybe. Maybe not. You're on hiatus. Adele is handling restocking the store. If I don't return the boys' phone calls, they'll chalk it up to my notorious absentmindedness."

"Good point," Lorena conceded. "However if I don't check in on a regular basis, Claire will call missing persons." She shivered. "I had a funny dream last night."

"What about?"

"Something Dave said to me before he died. I can't remember what it was and I know it's important." Lorena headed for the bathroom. "I hate it when a memory keeps tickling my mind and won't show itself."

"Ditto," Sherry agreed. "Let's fool the memory. We'll go shopping and ignore it."

"Yes. Shopping!" Lorena grabbed her clothes and dressed swiftly. "You always know the right thing to say."

"Let's start at Harrods," Sherry said. She fingered her purse. "Can you cash a couple of those checks and give me some British currency. I'll pay you back."

"Good idea. Let's hit up the gift shop and see if they have a map."

The desk clerk took three checks and gave Lorena a stack of bills. Lorena handed them to Sherry. "This is the prettiest money, but I have no idea how to read it."

Sherry flipped through the bills. "The ones with the Queen are five pounds. The brown ones are ten-pound notes. The smaller ones are ten shillings. You've got a hundred and fifty pounds here."

"You keep it. I've got lots more travelers' checks. I like them better than credit cards. Credit cards don't give you change."

Sherry grabbed several pamphlets on things to see and do in London. "After lunch we could go to Buckingham Palace or the Tower. You'll love that."

"Anne Boleyn and stuff?"

Sherry nodded. "And King Henry the Eighth's armor. He was a little man. I never knew that. The Plantagenet's were tall, but Henry was a Tudor."

They stepped out into the brisk morning air. Lorena consulted the map she'd purchased in the gift shop. "It's on Brompton Road in Knightsbridge. Looks like a four block walk."

They strolled along, peering in shop windows. Lorena stopped at a jewelry store. "I want to go in."

"Later." Sherry urged her along. "They have all that stuff in Harrods."

Harrods occupied a three-city block area. Windows shaded by green awnings gave a hint of the delights inside. They walked in and inhaled the wonderful department store smell. Perfume, new leather, and the unmistakable scent of luxury.

Lorena paused at the makeup department. "Let's start here."

A smiling blonde in a pink smock approached them. "We are doing a makeup demonstration of Elizabeth Arden products."

Lorena glanced along the mirrored counters, displaying jewel toned eye shadows and boxes of eyelashes. "I'm in," she said, moving to the tall stool located next to the counter. "Do me."

The salesgirl looked uncomprehending. Lorena laughed. "It's an American expression. It means please make me over."

The clerk's face brightened. "Excellent." She studied Lorena's complexion. "I think the 'glowing face' is ideal with your hair and skin type. It is a casual and informal look for daytime wear. Golden beige foundation, tawny peach rouge, translucent powder." She explained as she applied the products. "Beige eye shadow accented with brown eyeliner and false half-lashes. Coral-red lipstick with a light gloss."

Finally the lashes. Long and spiky. The girl applied them deftly and held up a mirror for Lorena to see.

Lorena gazed back at her reflection. Her face had been contoured and shimmered subtly. "I love it. I want it all." The salesgirl's eyes lit up. "Shall I add an eye cream for night and some make up remover?"

"Sure." Lorena chose two more shades of lipstick, and turned to Sherry who was smiling dreamy eyed at nothing in particular. "Focus. Jeremy won't run away. You're next."

Sherry obediently sat down in the vacated chair. She

eyed Lorena's makeup. "It's nice, but I want something different. Maybe a little less."

The sales girl complied. "This look is called the 'fragile face'. Off white foundation . . ."

Sherry closed her eyes and dreamed through the salesgirl's patter. She felt the hands moving over her face, creaming, stroking with feather light touches.

"It's a lovely look with your coloring." Emily held a mirror for Sherry.

Sherry eyed herself in the mirror. Her face had a porcelain look with faintly pink cheeks and pastel green eye shadow. Her eyes were outlined in sable brown and accessorized with feathery false eyelashes. Her lips gleamed shimmering coral. "I'll never get used to this," she whispered.

The sales girl frowned worriedly. "If you don't like it, I can do another look."

"No," Sherry assured her, "this is lovely." What would she think if I told her how old I really was? "I'll take everything."

Lorena returned with a flagon of Joy. "Can you hold all of this for me?" Lorena asked. "I have a lot more shopping to do."

"Of course, madam. If you like, we can have it delivered to your place of residence. May I inquire where you are staying?"

"The Cadogan. But you had better wait till I finish. I promise you there will be a lot more."

"We will hold your purchases behind the counter. I'll put them under my name. Ask for Emily."

Lorena smiled her thanks.

The stocking counter featured an array of legs in filmy rainbow colors. Sherry fingered a pair of semi-transparent tights. "Bone. An ugly name for a beautiful color. I used to have several pairs of these with bone colored shoes to match. I felt like the coolest girl on the planet."

"By all means, Oh cool one, let us buy bone." Lorena added a couple of pairs of black lace tights to their pile. "I was more of a black lace kind of girl."

They made their way to the lift. "I can't get used to live elevator operators," Lorena whispered, staring at the rotund man wearing a green and gold uniform. "It seems so weird." Lorena eyed the other passengers, taking note of outfits she liked.

"First floor," the lift operator called out. "Lingerie, Lady's Ready to Wear, Harrods Library . . ."

Lorena stopped listening. "If this is the first floor, what was the floor we came in on?" she asked.

"That was the ground floor." Sherry headed them to the lingerie department where Lorena pulled her forcibly away from a white Grecian nightgown with a black winged top of cobwebby lace.

"Necessities," Lorena reminded her. "Concentrate on bras and panties."

Sherry tried to concentrate on necessities, but her gaze drifted back to the nightgown.

"Lovely, isn't it? And you've got the figure for it," the firmly girdled saleswoman remarked. "Would you care to try it on?"

"Yes."

Lorena sighed and followed Sherry to the fitting room.

Sherry slipped the gown over her head, loving the slide of silk down her body. She lifted her arms to get the full effect of the sheer black lace sleeves.

"It's perfect."

Sherry saw Lorena smiling at her in the mirror.

"Sorry. I think I was jealous that you had someone who'd want to see you in it. I really miss that."

Sherry wished she could take away the shadow on Lorena's face. "Lorena, why don't you . . ."

"No. Not going there." She took the nightgown from Sherry. "I'll pay for this. Put your clothes back on. I want to hit *Ladies Ready To Wear.*"

I'm not ready for dresses," Sherry said. "I need sustenance."

Lorena regarded her with disapproval. "You have an appetite like an elephant. You never stop eating."

"That's why I like the English," Sherry agreed. "They eat six times a day. This will be our *elevenses.* That's what they call the meal between breakfast and lunch."

They stopped at the tearoom located near dresses. Sherry ordered scones, finger sandwiches, and the inevitable pot of tea.

Lorena poured herself a cup and glanced around, absorbing the ambience. "Does this place still exist in our time?"

"Lower your voice when you say things like that." Sherry took a quick look around to see if anyone was listening. "I think so, but who cares. We're here now."

"You're still planning to stay awhile, aren't you?"

Sherry nodded, her mouth full of sandwich.

Lorena looked resigned. "I think we'd better invest in warm coats."

Sherry picked out a burnt orange wool mini coat with horn buttons.

"Nice." Lorena handed Sherry a felt cloche in the same color. "You know what's funny? A lot of these fashions look like things you'd see in Beverly Hills in the present. Not the maxi coats, of course, but look at this one." She tried on a stunning black A line coat that ended above her knees. "Armani would be proud to claim it."

Sherry changed into a heather wool mini dress with flowing sleeves. "I'm dithering," she sighed, looking from a blue velvet Mary Quant to a flame-colored Halston.

"Take all three."

Sherry added Emma Peale pants, two blouses, and a fine wool sweater to her loot.

Lorena chose a couple of Givenchy knockoffs. Geometric A-line mini dresses, one in a bold crimson, the other a chaste black. "I can always dress them up." She also bought jeans and a couple of tight fitting turtleneck sweaters.

They skimmed the shoe selection, opting for sneakers and some small-heeled shoes with bows that looked like they might have come out of the Georgian period.

They stopped in the luggage department for suitcases. "I'd forgotten how heavy these were." Lorena said, hefting a beautiful tan leather bag. "I think I prefer bags with wheels."

"They haven't been invented yet."

"I wonder what would happen if I tried to fly home," Lorena asked.

"Nothing," Sherry said. "They'd take one look at your passport and put you in the clink. If you tried to tell them how you ended up with a passport that said good until 2019, they would move you to Bedlam."

"Is that a place? I thought it was a saying."

"It's a real place with a real honest to god mental hospital. We do *not* want to go there."

"Okay," agreed Lorena. "No airplane."

Sherry glanced at her wristwatch. "We need to hurry. Jeremy's meeting us at the hotel at one."

"Great. I live to play chaperone." Lorena caught Sherry by the hand. "Hon, are you sure you know what you're getting into? Falling in love and then losing it is hell."

Sherry's composure slipped. "Don't you think I know that? Tell me something. Would you have given up Dave if you knew he was going to die?"

"No." Lorena caressed the wedding ring she still wore. "No, I wouldn't have given up a second of it. Let's go meet your Jeremy.

Chapter 9

Jeremy rose from his seat in the lobby. "You look very snappy," he said, limiting himself to a kiss on Sherry's cheek. His fingers gripped hers as he turned to Lorena. "I hope you haven't finished all your shopping. My sister has a couple of places she'd like to introduce you to."

Lorena stuck her nose in the air. "Shopping is never finished, as any woman can tell you."

Sherry frowned at Lorena. *Play nice,* she mouthed.

"I thought I'd take you to a pub where Shakespeare used to hang out," Jeremy said, tucking them into the car.

"Really?" Lorena looked interested. "I thought they all burned in the Great Fire."

"The *Golden Hind's* outside that area. It would seem Will liked to travel."

Sherry and Lorena looked around at the oak beamed ceiling blackened with age. "Well if he didn't eat here, he ought to have," Lorena said.

Sherry caught sight of a flame red head. Jen. Locked into an argument with a noisy group seated at a large table which would have looked at home on the set of *Shakespeare in Love*. She tugged on Jeremy's arm and pointed her out. "What are the chances?"

"Excellent," he said in a voice meant for only her ears. "I knew they'd be eating here. I wanted to introduce her to Lorena in hopes they'd bond over shopping, which leaves us free to bond over something else."

He tapped Jen on the shoulder.

Jen turned around and scowled. "What are you doing here? Keeping tabs on me?"

"I dropped in to show Sherry and Lorena a historical sight."

Lorena stared at the man seated next to Jen. "I know you. Didn't we work together at Long Wharf?"

Sherry stepped on her foot.

Lorena realized what she'd said. "Sorry," she stuttered. "You remind me of an actor who played Benedict in . . . in a production I did in Rep. I played Hero" she gabbled. "It's a boring part. I'm much better suited to Beatrice, but I didn't get to play it until—Ow!"

"Lorena's always seeing people she thinks she knows," Sherry interposed, with a steely look at Lorena. "Comes of moving around so much." She smiled at Jen. "This is my friend Lorena. She's an actress too."

The dark curly haired actor Lorena had recognized stood up and kissed Lorena's hand. "If we don't know each other, I am sure that's an oversight on the part of the Universe. I've never played Benedict, but if I did, I would be honored to have you as Beatrice." He bowed and pulled out a chair. "John Luterman at your service. Won't you join us?"

Sherry enjoyed the sight of Lorena's flaming face. She rarely lost her equanimity.

"Yes, do." Jen nodded coolly. "We were discussing how bad Americans were at Shakespeare."

Lorena sat down. "That's funny," she said, in a voice like lemon ice. "We often have that same conversation in America. Only it's about how bad British actors are at doing American accents." She shook her head sadly. "Your attempts at Williams and O'Neil are appalling."

Jen fired up. "The American movie attempts at Shakespeare are a disaster. Julius Caesar with Marlon Brando as Brutus? Ridiculous! You should stick to American plays."

Lorena's eyes flashed murder. "Yes, well . . ." Her expression changed. "'The quality of mercy is not strained. It droppeth as the gentle rain from Heaven upon the place beneath,'" she recited in a crystal pure Oxford British accent. "On the other hand," she drawled in a magnolia rich southern voice, "y'all are pure dee awful when it comes to Williams."

John laughed. "Pax. You've proved your point. I want to go to America and work in theatre there. I suppose it would behoove me to learn some proper American dialects."

Jen stared at Lorena intently. "I need that accent. I've been looking for someone to coach me. We're rehearsing *A Streetcar Named Desire*. Come back to the theater with us."

Lorena looked at Sherry inquiringly.

"Go ahead, Lorena," Jeremy said. "I wanted to borrow Sherry for the afternoon."

Lorena and Jen both eyed him like disapproving mothers. Sherry stifled a giggle

Jeremy was the picture of injured innocence. "Honestly, Jen, do you think I'm going to take her to my flat and have my wicked way with her?"

I hope so, Sherry thought.

"This is strictly business. I have to interview Lady Dorchester this afternoon and I thought Sherry might be able to help."

"That old bat? She's barmy." Jen said. She turned to Sherry. "Better you than me. Good luck."

"Why does he need help interviewing her?" Lorena asked.

"She won't talk to him unless there is a woman present. She's totally off her rocker. Thinks she's still a lady in waiting."

"What's wrong with that?" Lorena asked.

"To Queen Victoria," Jeremy answered. "And she thinks her pet mouse is the reincarnation of Queen Victoria. I'm going to interview the mouse." He turned to Sherry. "You don't by any chance speak mouse? I could use a translator."

"I'm sorry," Sherry replied with a straight face, "the only mouse I was well acquainted with my s— ah . . . sister's pet mouse and he spoke common field mouse. I'm afraid I won't be much help."

Jeremy's eyes crinkled at the corners. "That's all right. We'll rely on Lady Dorchester."

"It's a castle." Sherry looked up at the sweeping edifice faced in brick and trimmed in white stone.

"Hampton Court. A lot of the grace and favor ladies have rooms here."

"Grace and favor." Sherry rolled the words on her tongue, enjoying the sound.

"Grace and Favor apartments are given to former ladies in waiting and other people who have done services to the crown."

Their footsteps echoed in the cobblestoned courtyard. Jeremy tucked Sherry's arm in his guiding them to the east wing. "She really was a lady in waiting to Queen Victoria, you know. Of course, that was seventy years ago."

Jeremy pushed the small buzzer. It had an ancient cranky sound. He turned and bracketed her face with his hands. "You know I would much rather have taken you to my flat to continue where we left off, but it's Mrs. Bridge's Day."

"Mrs. Bridge?" Sherry's breath caught as he brought his lips down to the pulse in her throat.

"My charwoman." He followed the line of her throat up to her lips. "I don't want an audience. I want you to myself."

The door creaked open.

Jeremy sighed and stepped away from her. "Good afternoon, Moulder. I believe Emma's expecting us."

The butler's translucent skin and wispy white hair contrasted oddly with his snowy linen and impeccably pressed cutaway coat.

"Her Majesty and Lady Dorchester are in the drawing room. If you would follow me, please." He turned and creaked away.

"Moulder?" Sherry whispered.

"I know," Jeremy said. "Never was a name more apt. Some things are serendipity."

The floor to ceiling windows shrouded in burgundy velvet curtains were a perfect frame for the tiny white haired lady sitting erect in a high back chair, her feet resting on a *petit pointe* footstool. On the table beside her sat a golden cage.

"Jeremy, you're late," Lady Dorchester said reprovingly. "I expected you quite half an hour ago. Promptness is a virtue you must try to acquire. Her Majesty doesn't like to be kept waiting."

Jeremy strode over to her and kissed her powdery cheek. "I'm sorry, Emma. Allow me to present Miss Sherry Southerland. Sherry, this is my godmother, Lady Dorchester."

Sherry gave into the urge to curtsey. "I'm honored to meet you, Lady Dorchester."

Lady Dorchester eyed her with bird bright eyes. "American, are you? Good strong blood in the colonies. You'll do nicely."

Jeremy sighed. "Emma, she's only just now met me. Give her a chance to know me before you make her run screaming." He turned to the golden cage and went down on one knee. He bent his head. "Your Majesty, please forgive my tardiness. I trust I find you in good health?"

Sherry's mouth dropped open. Through the airy golden bars she could see the back of the cage was painted to resemble a marble wall. A full-length portrait of Prince

Albert graced a miniature fireplace. A doll-sized saucer made of fine porcelain contained a wedge of cheese and a small seedy cake. The matching saucer looked to have tea in it.

A white mouse wearing a jeweled collar occupied the center of the cage. When she saw Sherry, she scurried behind a miniature sofa upholstered in red velvet.

"Fear not, Your Majesty. Miss Southerland is acquainted with others of your breed, er, ilk and is most anxious to know you better." He turned to Sherry. "Curtsey," he whispered.

Sherry sank into the best curtsey she could manage. "Your Majesty."

The mouse flicked her shell pink ears and climbed onto the sofa.

Lady Dorchester tapped Jeremy on the shoulder with the tip of her cane. "Her Majesty consented to this interview because she has a number of things to convey to you about the changes she wants made in Parliament." She handed Jeremy an embossed sheet of stationery.

Jeremy read down the list. "A woman Prime Minister? I don't think the country's ready for that."

"Your opinion is not required," Lady Dorchester snapped. "Your part is to publish her views in that magazine of yours."

Her Majesty fixed Jeremy with a black beady stare and twitched her whiskers. Sherry could almost hear her saying, "*We are not amused.*"

"*Twenty-Eight* will be most honored to publish this." Jeremy folded the paper carefully. "Now, if I could ask you a few questions about how you came to reside in your present form?"

"Really, Jeremy. One would think you had been born in a stable. One must never ask a lady about her age or appearance."

"Oh please," Sherry said. "I should so like to know how you found each other."

Lady Dorchester gave Sherry a benevolent smile. "I have a highly developed intuition. I can always see through to the true nature of things." She lowered her voice. "I woke up one morning and there she was, curled up on the bedside table in front of my miniature of Victoria and Albert. She opened her eyes and looked at me and I knew she was the reincarnation of the Queen."

The mouse squeaked imperiously.

"I had the cage built to her specifications." She glanced fondly at the mouse. "It's so lovely to have someone to talk to. Someone who knew me when I was young and remembers the same things I do."

"Yes, I can see that," Jeremy said, his tone gentle and respectful.

Moulder entered with a loaded tea tray. Jeremy sprang up to assist him. Moulder speared him with an icy look. "I'm quite capable of carrying out my duties, Master Jeremy. Please be seated."

Jeremy reached for Sherry's hand and seated them both on the Queen Anne loveseat.

Silence reigned as Moulder poured tea into delicate flower-sprigged Limoges cups and handed them round. He opened the cage and presented Her Majesty with a fresh seedy cake.

"Thank you, Moulder," Lady Dorchester said. "Lady Sherry can hand 'round the sandwiches."

"But I'm not a La . . ."

Lady Dorchester silenced her with a look.

"Very well, Ma'am." Moulder bowed and left the room.

"He remembers the old days when everyone who came through our doors had a title," Lady Dorchester explained. "He doesn't like changes."

Sherry offered her the platter of finger sandwiches.

Lady Dorchester's blue veined hands hovered a moment

and selected a watercress sandwich. "You're a sweet child. Very well mannered."

Her Majesty squeaked and nibbled on the seedy cake.

Lady Dorchester beamed. "Caraway has always been her favorite." She turned to Jeremy. "When do you plan to give up this nonsense and get back to your proper calling?"

"Never." Jeremy selected a cucumber sandwich and bit into it.

Lady Dorchester turned to Sherry for support. "Wouldn't you think a person who took a Masters in Physics at Oxford would want to put the degree to proper use instead of piddling around with a magazine?"

Sherry felt Jeremy tense. She turned to look at him. "You told me you'd read English."

"Double major," he said briefly. "I enjoy the magazine, Emma. I find amusing people to be far preferable to bombing them."

Sherry's mouth dropped open.

"You're making too much of that," Lady Dorchester said sharply. "It was one bomb and you didn't make it."

"The theory behind it came from my work." He smiled at Lady Emma. "Tell me more about Her Majesty."

"She's a grand old lady isn't she?" Jeremy turned up the car heater.

"You were wonderful with her," Sherry said. "Are you really going to publish Her Majesty's demands?"

"Of course. Here in England, we cherish our eccentrics." He sighed. "It's difficult to imagine what it must be like to outlive your generation."

Sherry had a swift flash of herself at ninety. What if it was only her and some pet and a bunch of memories? Her mouth tightened. Well, damn it. If she was left alone with a bunch of memories, she wanted them to be spectacular. She looked at Jeremy. What was she waiting for? "Do you think Mrs. Bridge is gone yet?"

The car jerked forward. Jeremy put out his arm to stop her from hitting the dashboard. "Sorry. Yes. She likes to be home before dark."

"Let's stop at the hotel so I can leave a note for Lorena."

Chapter 10

The hall smelled of lemon oil and fresh flowers.

"Alone at last." Jeremy slid her coat off her shoulders and hung it on the curved ironwork coat rack. "And to make sure . . ." he secured the chain on the door. "Now where were we last night before we were so rudely interrupted? Ah, I remember." He drew her into his arms and captured her lips, exploring, nibbling.

Sherry closed her eyes, savoring the feel of his lips on hers. Wanting more, she pulled him closer and deepened the kiss.

Jeremy broke away. "Not here," he said hoarsely. "Come with me."

Streetlamps cast a flickering light through the open curtains. The bed lay in gold shadows. Jeremy switched on the lamp on the nightstand. When he turned her into the light she could see her own need and desire reflected in his eyes.

"You are so beautiful. I have never wanted anything as much as I want you right now." He molded their bodies together, one hand warm and firm on the small of her back, the other cupping her neck. His lips caressed her eyelids and moved downward.

Sherry welcomed the rush of sensual heat. She wound her arms around his neck. Their lips fused. He tasted sweet and dark and wild.

Jeremy shuddered.

She felt his hands fumbling for the zipper of her dress. She loosened her embrace and allowed the dress to fall to the floor.

His body grew taut at the sight of her breasts barely veiled in white lace. He slipped down the satin straps. "Perfect."

The sensation of his warm tongue licking, touching, teasing, was almost unbearable. She rubbed herself against his erection trying to get closer. Her core was hot wet and ready, oh so ready. She wanted him inside.

She unbuttoned his shirt, feeling the pulse of his heart beneath his skin. His chest was smooth and lightly crisped with hair. She stroked his nipple with her tongue.

He gave a stifled moan, picked her up in his arms, and laid her on the bed. He swiftly stripped off the rest of his clothes. Steel muscles sheathed in velvet. Sherry's eyes fastened on the most important muscle.

"Oh, yes," she breathed.

He knelt between her outspread legs and slowly pulled down her last remaining barrier. His mouth trailed a path, warm, searing butterflies, from the breastbone to her pubis. He slipped a finger inside, teasing her with a delicious rhythm. The sound of his ragged breathing indicated his precarious control.

"Jeremy!" The beautiful pressure became unbearable. She surged to meet him.

Jeremy lowered his body to cover hers. His lips moved to her mouth, his kiss as slow and sensuous as his entry.

The velvet touch teased her, slipping slowly in and out with soft deliberate strokes. She breathed in the heat of his spicy scent, the steel muscles in his shoulders slick against her palms. Her need grew. "More." She grasped his buttocks pulling him deeper.

He grasped her hands and drew them above her head. "Not yet" His beautiful face showed the strain of the control he was exerting. He pulled out almost completely. He slid in again, and again and again, each thrust driving her desire higher and higher. His hand quested for the magic button and found it.

"Jeremy!" She arched with a scream of pleasure. "Don't stop. Please! Please come with me."

"Yes!" With one long thrust he filled her completely.

Her pleasure spiraled higher as he picked up the pace. There was no thought, only feeling. Only the gasps of two humans driven, meeting, mating.

"*Jeremy!*"

His answering shout echoed as she whirled upward, out of control, till she hit the stars with a bang.

Jeremy collapsed against her. Their mingled heartbeats sounded like a drum solo. He slowly eased out of her, resting his head on her breast. His rapid breathing eased.

Her nerveless hand came up and settled on his curls. Neither spoke. They stayed that way for what seemed like hours.

Their trance was broken by a loud honk from the street.

Jeremy sighed. "That was, without question, the most amazing sex I have had in my life. I may have died and gone to heaven."

Sherry felt rich and silky like a well-fed cat. She curled into him. "You know I love to read romances, but I never could believe them. The descriptions of the love often seemed so wild. I thought they made it up because I never felt anything like that."

She turned his face to hers. "I was wrong," she whispered. "I guess I had never met my prince." She breathed a butterfly kiss on each eyelid. "Hello, Prince."

He sought her lips, his eyes still closed. "Sherry Sutherland," he murmured, "I believe you are my heart."

The ring of a phone startled her. Sherry laughed. "I haven't heard a ring like that in years."

"Mmm. It's probably Jen. I'm not going to answer." Jeremy's eyes flew open. "Where have you been that you haven't heard a phone ring?"

"I hear phones all the time. Mine plays *Singing in the Rain.*"

Jeremy quirked an eyebrow. "Is that some new American invention? I want a phone that plays music."

Tripped again. She *had* to remember. 1969. Sherry reached up and smoothed away the slight frown between his eyes. "Sometimes I talk before I think. I was dreaming of . . . a story I read."

"Sounds interesting. Who's the author?"

Sherry felt like a butterfly pinned by his interested gaze. "I don't remember."

Jeremy stared at her intently. "There's a mystery in you, my love. Something I can't quite catch."

Sherry looked at him mutely. If only he'd let it go. More time. Please.

"Are you hungry?" He sat up. "Thirsty? A glass of wine? A cup of tea?"

"Not now." She snuggled back and pulled him to her. "I want to know more about you." Tell me about my prince."

"Nothing to tell. I'm not very interesting. When I'm not working I usually have my nose in a book. Science mostly."

"Why science?"

"I think it started with my first comic book, Simon and Kirby's *Race to the Moon.*" Jeremy's eyes held a far off look. "I wish I still had a copy of that. It was a corker. I became a science fiction junkie. Hence the double major. I couldn't decide whether I wanted to write science fiction or discover how to make it reality." He played with her hair, stroking it and winding it around his fingers. "I thought I would invent a better means of powering space ships. I wrote a paper on my discoveries about neutrons. Some chap used it to come up with a bomb that destroyed people instead of buildings. He cited my work as being critical to his invention."

"That's terrible. But it's not your fault."

"I know that, but I decided I wasn't up for any more discoveries. So I stopped, and took over the magazine from my father. He grumbles a lot about the direction I've taken it in, but he doesn't interfere."

He smoothed away the frown from her forehead. "There's too much crazy in the world. I don't need to add to it."

Sherry caught his finger and kissed it. "Where did you go to school?"

"Local grammar school. My parents didn't want me sent to boarding school. My mum thought it was medieval." Jeremy laughed. "I don't think Dad trusted that the boarding school could knock the nonsense out of me. He was very strict. Wanted to knock it out himself."

Sherry's eyes widened. "He *beat* you?"

"Not often. The only time I remember him taking a belt to me was when I set the house on fire. And that was an accident."

"The fire or the belt?" She stroked the corner of his mouth. "I think you dangled your participle."

"The fire, of course. I had Jen's doll tied to the stake, so of course there had to be a fire." He turned and straddled her. "I will have you know, my participle is not dangling. It feels ready for another round."

"Well I'd never want to disappoint a participle."

She suckled the nearest thing she could reach–his nipple. The result was most satisfactory. They loved softly, sweetly, with laughter and murmurs of appreciation. Time had no meaning. Slowly the sparks they made between them escalated into a firestorm. They rose from peak to peak till Sherry thought she would die from pleasure.

"Jeremy!"

Jeremy smothered her scream with a kiss and followed her over the edge. They fell asleep still holding hands.

Chapter 11

The first streaks of sunrise woke Sherry. She turned into the body of her lover. *Her lover.* What wonderful words. Bubbles of joy moved through her bloodstream. This is what she had been missing and now she had it.

But for how long? The rising sun shone directly in her eyes. She sat up to avoid the rays.

Jeremy rolled over and smiled at her, sleepily. "You look like you spent a wakeful night."

"Now is that a nice thing to say to an old lady?"

He laughed. "Are you fishing for a compliment?"

She smiled down at him; stroked his hair. "Yes." She wasn't ready to talk about where she came from, or more accurately . . . *when.*

In one lithe move, he jumped out of bed. "I am going to show you why you should stay with me. Wait here."

She lay back luxuriating in the feeling of the soft sheets on her body. She turned and caught sight of her tangled hair on the pillow. Tangled! She jumped up and made a run for the shower. The hot spray massaged her skin. She poured shampoo into her hands and breathed in the scent of lemon and something else. Rosemary?

She dried off and used his deodorant. Why didn't men use body lotion? She rubbed toothpaste on her finger and brushed her gums. Feeling minty fresh, she grabbed his robe from the back of the door and hopped back into bed.

Jeremy appeared in the doorway with a tray bearing tea accoutrements, a plate piled high with buttered toast, and a vase with a single purple aster. He set down the tray and offered her the vase. "I plucked it from the garden. It was the last one."

She surveyed his non-attire. "You went into the garden naked?

"No one saw me. It's the back garden and walled off. I didn't think it was a good idea to go on the street like this. Otherwise I would have brought you roses." He placed the tray between them and got back into bed. He poured her a cup of tea; offered her milk and sugar.

Sherry caressed his cheek, loving the prickle of whiskers against her fingertips. "You did this for me?"

"I wanted you to know how domesticated I was. If you move in with me, you can look forward to a lifetime of breakfast in bed."

Sherry bent her head over the tea, letting her still damp hair form a curtain between them. She needed to tell Jeremy the truth, but she couldn't think how to do it. Jeremy, I am sixty-three years old and I traveled here from the twenty-first century, and I met you again. How's that for a funny coincidence?

Yeah, right!

"Stay with me, Sherry."

Her fingers tightened around the hand he held out to her. She wanted to say yes so badly. "There is nothing I want more, but I don't think I can. I have obligations in America."

"When do you have to meet them?" He paled. "I never thought to ask. Are you married?"

"I am, at this moment, single, and I'll stay as long as I can." Two weeks. Two weeks was all she asked. Then she'd tell him.

"Thank you." She saw questions in Jeremy's eyes, but he didn't voice them. He glanced at his watch on the bedside table. "The time! Oh Lord. I'm late for work. I'd take the day off, but we go to press tomorrow."

He made a dash for the bathroom. She heard the shower running. Sherry took another sip of tea and nibbled on the toast. It was stale and heavily buttered. She smiled and sent him a happy thought.

She got up and explored his closet. There was a bar of suits; gray, navy, pinstriped, cloth, wool, worsted, jersey. A second bar held shirts, plain, striped, and one or two in flowered patterns. A spray of three racks held ties.

Jeremy came up behind her. The scent of his damp body made her feel dizzy. He picked her up and deposited her back on the bed.

"This is an emergency quick change and I can't have you getting run over." He snatched a white shirt and buttoned it up rapidly. He opened the drawer of the mahogany dresser and grabbed jockey shorts and black silk socks. He took the first suit that came to hand, a navy blue worsted three piece.

"Very conservative," Sherry praised. "You look like you are going to meet with a bank manager."

He shot her a crooked grin. "When you own a magazine that publishes stories about aliens abducting small children, you need to look professional at all times."

"Aliens?" Her heart lifted. If he could entertain the thought that a mouse was Queen Victoria, maybe he could believe her.

"Yes, and also three hundred pound cats and people who dine on trees."

"They do not."

"Perfectly true. There's this one old chap that fancies he is a beaver." He straightened his tie. "He is in the House of Lords." He looked in the leather box on top of the dresser and drew out two keys. "These are the keys to the flat. I'll be home by six and we'll go somewhere wonderful."

Sherry looked at the keys and her heart zoomed toward her stomach. "No. Wait. I meant I would stay here in London. I can't simply move in with you."

"Why not?" Jeremy did not look happy.

"Lorena. We came to London together."

"And?"

"I can't go tell her 'Hey, you know the guy I introduced you to yesterday? We've decided to move in together. So have fun and I'll see you whenever.' Best friends don't do that to each other."

"All right, then." Jeremy turned away, but not before she saw the hurt and anger in his eyes. "Game off." He put the keys back in the box. "Well, you have my card. Give me a ring at the office, if you'd like to get together."

"Don't be an ass." She got up and hugged his unyielding back. "Of course I want to get together."

"But you have Lorena to consider and there are your obligations in America. It's good to know where I stand in your regard." He turned in her arms and pulled her into a long intimate kiss that made her want to melt into a puddle on the floor. "Goodbye, Sherry." Jeremy's voice cracked. He looked as shaken as she felt. The door shut behind him.

Sherry stood staring at the door, bemused. She trailed back to the bed and sat down. She sipped at her now cooled cup of tea and stroked the maroon silk robe she'd borrowed, breathing in his scent.

Now what?

Chapter 12

Lorena surveyed Sherry critically. "I would have thought you'd look a bit happier."

"It's complicated." Sherry tossed her coat on the chair and headed for the bedroom.

Lorena trailed after her. "Aren't you going to ask me what I did after you dumped me?"

"Let me change first." Sherry pulled out fresh underwear, the Emma Peale slacks, and a periwinkle satin blouse from her new suitcase. She grabbed the bag containing her cosmetics purchases and stalked into the bathroom.

"You need tea," Lorena said. "I'll order a fresh pot."

"He handed me his card and said 'Call me at the office if you want to get together.' And *then*," Sherry said, "he kissed me senseless."

"The cad!" Lorena said. "What happened next?"

"He walked out."

"So wrong. He should have let you have the last word. That's a woman's prerogative." Lorena poured Sherry a second cup of tea. "Are you going to call him?"

"No! Yes. I don't know." Sherry grabbed an apple from the bowl on the coffee table and bit into it savagely. "So how was rehearsal?"

"Jen's very good. They all were. They need a lot more practice with the accent though. I made them a tape." Lorena rolled her eyes. "Reel to reel. Can you imagine? After rehearsal we stopped by here to see if you wanted to go to dinner and the theatre and I got your note." She smirked at Sherry. "We saw Olivier doing Rattle in *Way of The World*. He was awesome. I almost fell on the floor laughing. I'll go see it again, if you want to?"

"I'll think about it." Sherry tried to push Jeremy to the back of her mind. "So what would you like to do today?"

"I told Jen we'd meet her at the theatre after rehearsal. She gets out at five. She wants to take us shopping." Lorena moved to the window and stared down at the street. "I had another dream about Dave last night. He morphed into Tinkerbell shaking fairy dust on me. But there was something else . . . I wish I could remember what."

"Let's go to Kensington Gardens," Sherry suggested. "That's where Peter Pan used to hang out. There's a statue of him there I'd love to show you. Maybe Tinkerbell will appear and nudge your memory."

"Sounds like a good way to spend the morning," Lorena said. "Let's stroll through the park and ogle guys." She grinned at Sherry. "And for the first time in decades I know they'll ogle us back. Looking twenty rocks."

"This is glorious," Lorena said, looking up at the scarlet, gold, and orange canopy of branches arching over them.

"Mmm," Sherry agreed, glad of her warm coat in the snap of tangy November air.

Dried leaves drifted across the lush green lawns and crunched under their feet as they walked along the serpentine toward Kensington Gardens.

Lorena stopped in front of a statue of a small boy in a ragged tunic blowing on a thin reed pipe. He stood on top of a jagged rock so shiny that it looked like a waterfall. She pulled out her iPhone to snap a picture.

"Put that away! It's hasn't been invented yet."

"Oops." Lorena dropped the iPhone back in her purse. She looked around to see if anyone noticed. A man in a snap-brim capped winked at her. She smiled at him and turned back to Sherry. "I'm counting that guy as an ogler." She looked up at the bronze mountain etched with images of fairies and other strange and wonderful things. "I wish I had an old Kodak. I wanted you to take my picture in front of it." "Did you see that Johnny Depp movie about J. M. Barrie and the four children that inspired Peter Pan?" Sherry asked. *"Finding Neverland?* Yeah. Dave and I went on our anniversary. Dave told me that in real life, J M Barrie took photographs of the boy, Peter, in a special Peter Pan costume he designed. The sculptor used the pictures to model this statue. I asked him how he knew that and he said . . ." Lorena stopped, her brow furrowed.

"What?" Sherry asked.

"Damn! I hate it when that happens. I can't grab the memory." Lorena looked frustrated. "My body got young, but my brain's still sixty-four."

They sat on a park bench near the statue. "I always thought I'd find Neverland someday," Sherry said. "Maybe that's my problem. I'm still looking for the fairy tale ending." She crossed her arms over her heart. "I wish there was one."

Lorena didn't respond. She sat staring at the statue, fingers drumming on her purse. "Sherry, that lost thought of mine? I think it's important. I need to go back."

"Where?"

Lorena pulled Sherry to her feet. "I want to get a cab and go to that pub where we met Jeremy. I need to see if the doorway is still there."

"No." Sherry's heart raced "You agreed we'd stay. You promised."

"I don't mean we have to use the gate right now. I want to see if it's still there. Come on. Please?"

Sherry shook her head. She felt like an over-wound spring.

"And after we check on it," Lorena said persuasively, "maybe we could find that place Jane from the shop told us about. You know the French one."

"Cromaniere's."

"How did you remember that?"

Sherry attempted a smile. "I'm not the one losing her thoughts."

"Oh that's right. Make fun of the elderly." Lorena hailed a cab. "Shakespeare's pub."

The driver gave her a sardonic look. "Care to make a bet on exactly how many pubs in the greater London area are named Shakespeare's? Popular name, that. Could you be a bit more specific, luv?"

Lorena rooted in her handbag and came up with a pack of matches. "Two Hundred Ten Argyle Street," she announced. "Corner of Argyle and Greater Marlborough Street." She turned to Sherry. "Don't you love that? *Greater* Marlborough Street! Gotta love the English. Wonder where *Lesser* Marlborough Street is?"

The cab jerked forward throwing them back against the seat. They righted themselves and stared out the windows.

"It's disconcerting driving on the wrong side of the road," Lorena observed. "It feels like my world is askew."

The cab stopped in front of Shakespeare's. Sherry paid the driver.

The street looked different when devoid of the romance of fake gas lighting. The daylight accentuated the shabby.

Lorena led the way to the shop where they had been the night before and scrutinized the window. "Same shop. Different dress."

"Fine. We're in the right place." Sherry took in the outrageous purple dress that looked as if it were made from tissue paper. "You need to try that dress on."

"Stay focused. The doorway was on the other side of the street two or three doors down."

Sherry bit back an acerbic reply and followed her across the street. The doorways had green or brown wooden doors all featuring cracked peeling paint. None of the doors had knockers.

"They all look alike," Lorena muttered. "How are we going to find it?"

They walked to the end of the block. Nothing. They headed back toward the dress shop. None of the doors looked familiar.

Now Sherry started to get nervous. "We must have missed it. It's got to be here."

"Okay, we start again." Lorena peered at the metal frame on the side of the door. "This time we'll read all the names."

The first two doors yielded nothing. Tiny typed names and apartment numbers. Some of the spaces were blank. They started to read the third door, Number 217. All the spaces were blank except one. In neat typed blue ink it read **The Castle. Please use ticket.**

Lorena spotted an inconspicuous credit card sized slot near the doorknob and gave a sigh of relief. She fished out her ticket and slid it in. The slot lit up. The lock clicked. "Yes!" She turned the handle. The door swung outward. Inside was a second door with a sign above it, *Final Exit.* The slot on the door glowed dimly. Lorena started to insert her ticket.

Sherry snatched it out of her hand. "Not. Yet!"

"Sheesh! Chill." Lorena scowled. "You didn't have to grab it. I said I'd stay."

"Here now. Wot's going on? Is this lady bothering you, Miss?"

Sherry swung around and found herself nose to nose with a row of brass buttons. Her eyes traveled upward to the black chin strapped helmet. She turned to Lorena and handed her back the ticket. "Help," she mouthed.

Lorena stepped out of the hallway and closed the door firmly behind her. "Sisters." She looked up into the Bobby's ruddy face and fluttered her eyelashes. "We're always fighting about something. Thank you for coming to my rescue. We'll just . . ."

"Americans, are you?" The Bobby's eyes remained impassive. "I saw you going up and down the street and I thought you might be lost."

"Well, yes. A bit." Lorena turned up the wattage on her smile. "We're supposed to meet, ah, Lord Bothwell at Cromaniere's, but I think we took a wrong turn. Could you direct us?"

He turned and pointed in the direction of Shakespeare's. "Bottom of the street. Turn left. You can't miss it."

"Thank you. Sergeant. Cheerio." Lorena seized Sherry's arm and propelled them briskly down the block.

Sherry thought she could feel the Bobby's eyes boring into her back. "Lord Bothwell?" she questioned.

"I was going for respectable with a touch of class. Slow down. We'll don't want to look like we're fleeing."

They continued down the street at a slower pace. As they turned the corner, the wind blew up. Clusters of dry leaves whirled in miniature tornados.

Sherry spotted a green awning with Cromaniere's in dull gold lettering on the opposite side half way down the block. Ficus trees in large flowerpots flanked the entrance. A second set of flowerpots had actual flowers in them. As they drew close Sherry caught the scents of lavender and mignonette. "Nice."

The doorman for the restaurant came to attention. He bowed and ushered them inside. The maître d's vinegary smile expressed his opinion of their social station. He led them to a table in the back, near the kitchen.

Lorena drew herself up and stared at the table in disbelief.

Sherry smiled inwardly. It had been a long time since anyone had shown Lorena to the back of a restaurant.

"Not that one." Lorena's voice rang out imperiously. "No one is sitting at the front table by the window."

The maître d' looked down his nose at her. "I am sorry madam, but that table is unavailable. It is reserved."

Lorena marched over to the table and plucked the reserved sign off it. She handed it to the maître d'. "Not any more. You can put this on another table."

The maître d' started to say something, but quailed before Lorena's dominating stare.

He surrendered to the inevitable, bowed, and walked away.

Lorena picked up the menu. "Snobby guy. Nice place. Oh! I want the French onion soup."

Sherry frowned over the tiny script. "I wish I spoke French." She scanned the menu looking for words she knew. "All I recognize is *Salade Verte*." She shut the menu. "I give up. You order." She caught the glint of fun in Lorena's eyes. "And no tricks. If you order snails I'll . . ."

"You'll what?" Lorena asked sweetly.

"I'll drop them in your lap. And then I'll order a Ginger Beer."

"You're such a spoilsport." Lorena gave their order in a spate of liquid French which seemed to make the waiter very happy.

The sommelier appeared with a bottle of wine swaddled in a snowy linen napkin. He uncorked it and poured her a small glass. Lorena took a sip. She closed her eyes and rolled the wine around on her tongue, then nodded graciously at the sommelier. He filled their glasses.

Lorena reached for a breadstick. "I wasn't planning to leave you. Remember that sparky light when we went through the door? I started worrying that our being here was some kind of computer glitch."

Sherry sampled the wine. It slid down her throat leaving a warm mellow trail. "And now? Going back to the door satisfied you that it wasn't?"

"No. I still think it must have been a glitch, but I didn't smell any burnt wires. However it happened, I believe we can go home. That's what I was worried about. I had visions of having to click my heels three times without the benefit of ruby slippers."

Sherry grinned at the mental image of the two of them holding hands, chanting. 'There's no place like home'. "Maybe it's easier for me to believe in time travel because I read a lot more science fiction than you. And a lot of what I've read has already come true. The world has nuclear subs, and Jules Verne thought of them first. Star Trek's automatic doors have been commonplace for decades. Time travel's been true in the Sci-Fi community forever. Even Mark Twain wrote about it in *A Connecticut Yankee in King Arthur's Court*."

"I loved *Connecticut Yankee*. But generally I prefer reading about real science to Sci-Fi."

"You do?"

"Don't give me that wide eyed stare. Yes, the blonde reads something besides scripts." Lorena bit off the end her bread stick. "These are great. Try one." She offered the breadbasket to Sherry. "I do love when science fiction becomes fact because it's usually in a much weirder way. Lots of writers wrote about landing on the moon. No one wrote about landing on the moon as being watched by the entire world on television, as brought to you by Tang, The Drink of the Astronauts. Or Brillo, the better scouring pad— 'Write in for your free Brillo Moon Map'. But that's what happened."

"I was here when they landed 1969. My whole office watched it on TV." Sherry frowned in thought. "I don't remember those ads though."

"I was visiting my family in Ohio." Lorena stared at her glass morosely. "Not so much fun. Hensley was like a time warp. Nothing ever changed. We watched the moon landing on our sixteen-inch black and white TV." She pushed away the breadsticks and motioned the Sommelier forward. "The thing is, Sherry, while this a lovely adventure, London in the sixties doesn't feel like my time and place."

"Okay, I'll bite. What is your place and time?"

Lorena shrugged. "It's one of those 'I'll know it when I see it' things, I think." She pondered for a moment. "Well, I wouldn't mind trying a trip to the moon. I made a reservation for one in 1954. It was in the back of an Action comic book. I'm guessing that one's not up for grabs."

"If you could change your life in any way, where would you branch off?"

Lorena smiled wryly. "There's only one thing I'd change and it's not changeable." She sipped her wine. "Now if I could take a trip to the moon . . . Of course my big ambition was Venus."

"You keep harping on space travel. Why?"

"Well it always seemed so odd to me." Lorena's eyes dreamed inward. "In the 1950s we knew we were going to the moon. In 1969, we actually did it. Then everything sort of stopped. It's been over forty years since we landed on the moon and almost nothing has happened since. It seemed the whole world lost interest in space travel. I never understood it."

Sherry leaned forward conspiratorially. "Maybe it was the mysterious 'Guardians of Outer Space.' Maybe they hypnotized the entire human race to keep us out of the game. Could be they didn't want such warlike creatures on the loose in the universe."

Lorena didn't laugh. "You might be right. It's weird when you think about it. 'Guardians of Outer Space' is as good an explanation as any."

Their food arrived. Sherry sniffed appreciatively. The salad was a bouquet of vegetables and herbs glistening with tiny drops of oil and red wine vinegar.

Lorena inserted her spoon past the Gruyere into the soup. She sipped the rich oniony broth. "This is bliss."

Silence reigned as they concentrated on their food. After the waiter removed the first course, Lorena continued. "Dave told me he listened to the moon landing on his car radio. He was driving back to Los Angeles from Santa Barbara." Her eyes lit up. "I would love to have seen Los Angeles in 1969. The Brown Derby was still there. You know the real one shaped like a hat?"

The waiter returned bearing a tray with two silver domed dishes. He placed a dish in front of each of them and whipped off the covers with a flourish. *"Voyez votre agneau de rôtis avec les pommes de terre frite minuscules."*

Lorena smiled at him. *"Aucun merci. Il semble divin. Merci beaucoup."*

The waiter looked at Lorena adoringly and bowed himself away.

Sherry grinned at Lorena. "I got the 'thank you' part twice. What else did you say?"

"I said the meal looked divine." Lorena picked up her fork and carved a small bite of lamb. "Yum. I was right."

Sherry giggled "I need to learn to speak French. I thought he was propositioning you." She tasted one of the tiny Pomme Frites. "Not only do the French sound sexy, they cook like gods. You should seriously consider a Frenchman as your next husband."

"There isn't going to be a next husband." Lorena shoved her plate away. "There are perfect things. You don't get to do those twice."

Sherry put her hand over Lorena's. "Come on. Talk to me. You rarely mention Dave any more. That's not good for you. Tell me about the beginning. Where did you meet?"

Lorena's hand tensed under Sherry's. "Mackinac Island, Michigan. 1972." She gave a tiny smile. "Gene Stratton Porter's books made me want to see that place, so when a dinner theatre job came up there, I took it."

"And?" Sherry prompted.

Lorena picked up her wine glass, then put it down and stared past Sherry's shoulder. "I was sitting on the boardwalk after the show, enjoying the ambiance and this guy came up to me and offered me some cotton candy. He had the warmest funniest brown eyes. That's what I noticed first. His eyes. He wasn't the most handsome guy I ever saw. Before . . . all my crushes had been blue-eyed blondes. When I looked into his eyes though, I knew I had been wrong. I liked brown hair and a lanky build and warm brown eyes. He smiled at me and . . ."

Lorena's smile wavered. "I know it's cliché, but I'd never felt like that before. Here was this stranger and I let him give me cotton candy. He shared a bench with me. Fingers sticky, mouths laughing. We sat and talked till the light dimmed. He walked me back to my room."

"And?"

"And nothing. The next day when I got up and looked out the window, he was there. Waiting. He had a bicycle built for two. He said he'd forgotten to ask me for my phone number, so he came back to wait for me. I invited him in for coffee, packed us a picnic lunch, and we bicycled around the shoreline. When we got tired, we stopped at a park and ate sandwiches and talked a lot more. Turns out he had reservations to the moon from the same comic book I had."

Lorena sighed. "He was a great kisser. Pretty soon we were doing a lot more than kissing. He asked me to marry him."

"That fast?" Sherry was enchanted.

Lorena nodded. "We were married a month later. It wasn't a big wedding. I told my mom. I did not want to be married in a church. David started teaching English at a high school in Portage, Michigan. It was a college town. Small and green and wonderful. But any place would have been wonderful with Dave." She looked blindly out the window, willing back tears. She took a deep calming breath. "Okay, that's enough about me."

The waiter wheeled over a dessert cart. Lorena chose something with pureed chestnut.

Sherry selected two tiny éclairs. She toyed with her demitasse, wondering what Jeremy was doing. Lorena's words echoed in her head. *Any place would have been wonderful with Dave.* That's how she felt about Jeremy. She pushed away the éclairs. She had to stop thinking about him.

The waiter presented the check. Sherry estimated a tip and pulled out the money to cover it. "What now? Buckingham Palace or the Tower of London?"

"The Tower. Can we take one of those big busses? I have always wanted to do that."

Chapter 13

The Tower proved a shock to Lorena. "I thought it would be a tower. It's a palace with a whole bunch of buildings and look at those birds!"

"Ravens" Sherry said. "I read there is a legend that as long as raven's nest in the White Tower, that there will always be an England . . . or something to that effect."

"They are as high as my knee. They are the biggest damn ravens I ever saw."

"Well, they take great care of them. They don't want to take a chance on them moving."

Lorena opened her pamphlet. "The Tower of London, created by William the Conqueror, is the oldest palace, fortress, and prison in Europe." She glanced at Sherry. "Prison. That's the part I remember. Wasn't Sir Walter Raleigh jailed there?"

Sherry nodded. "And Henry VII had two wives beheaded on Tower Green. Anne Boleyn and Katherine Howard."

Lorena continued reading. "It has been the repository of the Crown Jewels." She closed the pamphlet. "Let's start with the jewels. I love glitz. It says they are in the Wakefield Tower."

Lorena craned her neck past the velvet rope barrier guarding the plethora of crowns. "I wish we could get closer."

"That is so not about to happen."

"The names of the jewels sound like romance titles," Lorena said, reading the placards. "*Second Star of Africa,* the *Black Prince's Ruby, the Stuart Sapphire, St Edward's Sapphire,* and *Queen Elizabeth's Pearls.* I think I'll take up novel writing."

Sherry tried to imagine Queen Victoria wearing the crown, but all her mind's eye showed her was a mouse in a jeweled collar. She wondered if Jeremy had finished his article yet.

Lorena looked over at the guardsman in their red and gold uniforms standing nearby. "What do they call them?"

"Beefeaters."

"Why?"

"Who knows? I think they all look like King Henry the VIII." Sherry leaned over and whispered. "They all have to live in here, you know. All the guardsmen live somewhere in the towers."

Lorena looked startled. "That's bizarre. What if they have families?"

"The families live here too. They live in unused towers and converted stables. It's like its own very unmodern little village."

Lorena inhaled the damp mossy smell of the crenellated stone walls. "Somehow *Home Sweet Home* and *The Tower of London* in the same sentence make me think of *The Twilight Zone.*"

They followed a guide over to the White Tower marveling at all the armor and the little pockets of history.

"You were right. He was tiny," Lorena said, surveying King Henry VIII's suit of armor. "That armor looks about right for an eight-year-old."

By the time they visited the *Royal Beasts,* the *Scaffold site,* and *Traitors Gate* they were both wilting.

"Enough." Lorena eased her foot out of her shoe and rubbed the instep against her calf. "I'm sighted out and my feet hurt. Let's go find some tea."

"I want to buy some postcards," Sherry protested. "I want to send them to the boys."

"Get real, Sherry! They aren't born yet."

Sherry's heart skipped a beat. It felt like her brain was crossing. "I keep forgetting when we are. I mean, it all feels like now." She wanted to call Jeremy. "Let's go back to the hotel." Opening her purse she looked at the dwindling pile of notes. "I guess we can take a cab."

The message slipped under their hotel door was brief. *I'm sorry. Please call.*

Lorena shook her head. "You've got it bad, friend. You look like you're about to sprout wings."

Sherry dug through her purse for Jeremy's card.

Lorena kicked off her shoes and groaned in relief. "Let me call room service first and order tea. Then I'll go buy a paperback at the gift shop and give you some privacy. Hope they don't mind stocking feet."

Sherry knew she was smiling like an idiot and didn't care. "All right."

The brisk voice on the phone had a hint of Cockney in it. "He's unavailable right now. Can I take a message?"

"No, thanks. I'll call later," She hung up and dialed his home number. It rang several times before she remembered answering machines hadn't been invented yet. She heard the click of a key in the lock.

"What's wrong?" Sherry asked. "You look like the paparazzi are chasing you."

"We have to leave." Lorena seized her suitcase and started flinging in clothes "Now."

Sherry froze. "What are you talking about?"

"I was thumbing through the magazines wondering why they didn't have *People* and I remembered. I have an interview with *People* tomorrow." She grabbed her cosmetics from the bathroom and tumbled them in with the clothes. "I have to go back."

"I can't leave. I have to talk to Jeremy." Sherry took her own Harrods' purchases and folded them mindlessly into the other suitcase. "I can't go," she whispered under her breath.

"If I don't show up, my publicist will start a manhunt." Lorena sat on her bag to wrestle it closed. "No one misses an interview with *People* unless they're dead."

"Wait. It's not going to close with all that stuff hanging out. Here, let me." Sherry hefted the case onto the bed, emptied it, and repacked, folding each garment into a tiny roll. Tucking the cosmetics into crevices between the clothes, she snapped the case shut.

"Thanks." Lorena grunted as she eased her feet back into her shoes. "Let's go."

"I'm not finished packing," Sherry protested. "Go down to the desk and ask them to make up our bill. I'll be there in a minute."

"Good idea." Lorena hauled her suitcase off the bed. "I'll ask them to send up a bellhop. This thing is heavy."

As soon as the door closed behind Lorena, Sherry ran for the phone. "Please be there," she mumbled. She counted nine interminable rings. She hung up and tried the office number again.

The same pleasant cockney voice answered on the second ring. "*Twenty-Eight Magazine.* How may I direct your call?"

"Is Mr. Smythe back yet?"

"I'm sorry. He's left for the day. May I take a message?"

"Yes. Please tell him that Sherry Southerland . . ." She heard a knock at the door. *Jeremy!* "Never mind. Thank you." She hung up and raced to the door.

The bellboy's freckled face beamed up at her. "I've come for the bags, Ma'am."

Sherry felt like a pricked balloon. "Of course."

Jimmy lifted the suitcases on to his rolling cart and rang for the elevator.

Sherry took a last look round their suite and followed him. She came up to the desk as Lorena ripped out the last traveler's check to sign it.

"That's it?" Sherry whispered to her in shock.

Lorena nodded grimly. "It's good we're leaving now." I hope we've got enough left to pay the taxi."

Sherry rifled through her purse for the money Lorena had given her. "I've still got twenty pounds."

The desk clerk returned with four one-pound notes and their passports. "We are sorry to see you go, Mesdames. We hope you enjoyed your stay." He gestured to Jimmy who took their luggage to the entrance. The doorman whistled up a cab.

Lorena smiled and tipped them both before stepping into the cab. "Two Hundred Ten Argyle Street, please."

Sherry stared unseeingly out the window. She couldn't let it to end like this. She needed to let Jeremy know how much she loved him and why she couldn't stay.

When they got to Shakespeare's, Lorena tapped the cabdriver on the shoulder. "We need to go three doors down on the left."

The cabby pulled up in front to the shabby building and helped them out with their suitcases. Sherry started to pay him, hesitated for a moment. "No. Put my case back in the cab, please. I'll be right back."

Sherry followed Lorena to the door and watched her insert the ticket. The door opened.

Lorena slid the card into the second door and it swung back. She turned to Sherry. "Close the door. Where's your suitcase?"

"Here's what you're going to do." Sherry handed Lorena her American Express card. "Go back in and buy two more tickets. I don't want to take a chance on running out of money before I'm ready to leave."

Lorena looked at her as if she had lost her mind.

Sherry pushed her through the second door. "Do it! I'm going to stay right here and keep the door open."

She turned and smiled at the cabby. "It will only take a few minutes. I'll be right here where you can see me."

The cabby lifted his cap, scratched his head, and nodded resignedly. He reached in and snapped the meter back on. "Clock's ticking, miss."

"That's good." Sherry turned to Lorena. "Hurry."

Lorena scowled at her, turned, and disappeared down the hall. It seemed an eternity to Sherry before she reappeared.

Sherry's stomach rocketed to her feet. Lorena's features had phased back to her modern self. Sherry stroked a hand down her own face to check. Still silky smooth and unlined.

"Thank you," Sherry said with heartfelt gratitude.

Lorena stayed inside the door while she handed Sherry back her credit card together with a pamphlet. "I grabbed this at the desk while I waited. It's very interesting."

Sherry skimmed the pamphlet. "There's nothing in here about time travel."

"Take a look at the fine print." Lorena pointed to the bottom of the page.

Sherry shook her head. "I'd need a magnifying glass to read that in this light."

"The fine print absolves them of all responsibility for unforeseen circumstances."

"Time travel is an unforeseen circumstance?"

"I talked to surfer boy. He said if you choose to go to a place that you have strong memories or thoughts about, the game can get a little too real. He called it the *Time and Again Effect*." Lorena frowned. "I got the feeling I wasn't the first person to ask about it." She handed Sherry the ticket and the sheaf of traveler's checks. "The checks are in your name. I expect to see you home in two weeks."

Sherry opened her mouth to protest.

Lorena forestalled her. "No. I don't want to come back. Look, Sherry, this was fun, but 1969 London isn't my place." Her eyes lit with mischief. "Who knows? I may decide to try another time. In any case, if you're not back in fourteen days, I'm coming after you. Now give me his address."

Sherry rooted through her purse again and pulled out the piece of paper she had written Jeremy's address on. "Here take it. I have it memorized."

Lorena shook her head. "At our age we have energy saver light bulbs in our brains. It might take you a while to remember." She took out her checkbook and copied down the address on a deposit slip.

"Are you sure?" Sherry asked. "We could have a lot of fun. There is so much more to see."

"Yeah, yeah." Lorena pushed Sherry out of the doorway. "Go. Enjoy. Be careful."

The black door shut. The ticket slot glowed dimly and winked out. Sherry straightened her shoulders and returned to the cab. "Twenty-five Saint James Place, please."

She leaned back and stared out the window at the lamp lit street. She relegated Lorena to the back of her mind.

Jeremy.

Chapter 14
Lorena

Lorena stared at the closed door with a flicker of regret. Oh well, it had been fun while it lasted. Dratted interview. She loathed the things. She turned to pick up her suitcase and sighed as she thought of the contents. It wasn't as though she could wear them in this time. "Of course you can," she scolded herself. "You can bring 1969 back into fashion."

Her black cashmere coat felt good in the California November damp. Fog was coming in. She breathed in the smell. She thought about how Dave would have loved London. Her heart dropped back into the familiar hollow place. Something was missing. It was always missing since Dave died. Shrugging off the familiar pain, she threw the suitcase into the car and reached into the glove compartment for a cigarette. She lit up and drew in the smoke, relishing its harshness.

She sincerely loved her daughter. She knew she was blessed with friends, but it wasn't the same. When Dave died the only thing that kept her on this earth was her daughter and her new grandson. Sometimes she thought she could see Dave in his eyes.

"You promised," she said through stiff lips. "You promised we would grow old together. You said you would never leave me." The pain was almost unbearable. She took a deep drag on the cigarette to force the pain away.

At home she switched on the lights and took in, without appreciating, the tranquility of the craftsman style living room, with its warm white plaster walls. It echoed with emptiness.

She trailed her fingers along the top of Dave's favorite recliner. It was upholstered in French blue suede. He'd joked with her when she did it. "You can have your comfort but I want some style," she'd answered. She ought to get rid of it, but she couldn't bear the thought.

She'd put away his books and the parade of pictures that used to line the mantelpiece. Pictures of their life together.

The mantle was less crowded now. There was Claire and Jeff's wedding picture and of course, Dylan. Her chubby four-year-old grandson laughed back at her from the homemade frame he had decorated with his handprints. She smiled back at it. The world was okay. It could be better. But it was okay.

The pictures of her and Dave had been replaced by a pewter fairy, intricately carved with a dreamy expression on her face. The fairy held in her hand an opalescent glass horn. The horn of elf land.

Lorena crossed over to the blinking message machine on the glass covered side table. She frowned and cleared the automated message from some credit card company. What was the point of putting yourself on a do not call list if they still called. She listened to her agent's and her publicist's messages about the *People* interview at noon and mentally reminded herself to set an alarm. Claire's voice floated out. "Hi, Mom. Are we still on for tomorrow? Dylan wants a play date. Pick you up at three. All right?"

She went into the kitchen and made a cup of herbal tea. The scent of spearmint tickled her nostrils. What was Sherry doing right now?

Lorena sighed. She was happy for Sherry. Happy she had found someone even if it was only for two weeks. That was better than nothing. Sherry's ex-husband was a jerk. He'd done the predictable thing—turned forty-five and ran off with a twenty-something in his office.

What was wrong with men? They had such a thing about staying young, as if old age was a death sentence. It felt like sympathetic magic. They didn't want to get old so they surrounded themselves with the young and flashy.

Not Dave though. He'd never looked at another woman. It had been that way from the moment they met. They were the center of each other's universes. The familiar tightness seized her chest. She willed it away. She looked up at the picture of Claire. She remembered the day she was born and the look of awe and wonder in Dave's eyes as he cradled their tiny daughter.

The scene changed in her mind to her last memory of that hospital. The day Dave died. The too cold room smelled of antiseptic, mingled with the scent of roses. Lorena didn't care what the nurses thought. She had climbed into the bed with him. She wanted to hear and feel his every breath. She willed the monitor to keep beeping.

"Time is a funny thing," he whispered. "But it's never long enough."

She nodded, unable to speak for fear of screaming. His eyes clouded. The rhythm of his breath changed. The monitor sped up.

"Letter," he gasped. "Scrapbook. Under our wedding picture. Find it." He smiled at her. "Say hello to Peter Pan for me."

His eyes closed. The monotone of the single noted beep started.

He was gone.

She stayed in the room as his body grew colder, hoping it was a mistake. Trying to find him in that cold shell. They had to tear her away.

In the end they sedated her. The funeral and the interment were a blur. Something to be gotten through without screams. Her face became a mask. She comforted Claire and Jeff.

She spoke the right words to family and well-wishers. But she was not fully present. Some part of her spirit quested, searching for the other half of her soul.

The house phone rang. She set down the tea and picked it up.

"Hey, Mom. Why weren't you answering your cell phone today? I called several times. I finally resorted to leaving a message on your landline."

"Ah, I must have forgotten to charge it. How's Dylan?" she asked, hoping to forestall any further questions. "Did he do anything cute today?"

Claire giggled. "Oh, Mom, you are such a grandma. He loves that Superman costume you gave him. It's hard to peel it off him to take a bath. He told me he was going to marry Lois Lane and live next door to us."

Lorena laughed. "That's my boy. Dream big." Her thoughts drifted for a moment. She caught the tail end of Claire's sentence. "At preschool tomorrow around three. I need you."

"Of course I'm free." Wait a minute. What had she agreed to?

"We're having this program with stories and crafts and Dylan wants you to do crafts with him. Then comes the scavenger hunt and Dylan says you need to be his partner."

"Aren't they a little young to be doing scavenger hunts? Don't you have to be able to read to do that?"

"Yeah. That's why he needs you. Every kid is partnered with a grownup."

"Fine. I will be honored to be Dylan's partner." She felt a little glow in the area of her heart. Dylan loved her. He needed her. He was a piece of the chain tying her to the here and now.

"I have to go. I don't want to miss *Dancing with the Stars*. I love you, Mom." The dial tone beeped.

Good. She'd avoided the question. She wasn't ready to tell anyone where she'd been. London had been fun. And god, it had been nice to be young again. She touched her face. She could feel the wrinkles, the dry slightly powdery skin around her eyes. She went into the bathroom, switched on a light and looked in the mirror. The false eyelashes were still in place. The returned wrinkles cracked the 1969 *autumn face* makeup. Bronze shadows pooled in the creases of her eyes.

Lorena leaned over and carefully peeled off the lashes, wincing at the adhesive's tug. She went back to the living room and burrowed through her purse to see if the eyelash case had survived the time trip. It had. So had the autumn coral frosted lipstick. She went back to the bathroom and placed the lashes on the curve of the plastic plate.

She dabbed makeup remover on a cotton ball and erased the remnants of the autumn face with slow, careful strokes. She lathered up the green tea soap sniffing appreciatively at its scent, slicked it over her skin, and rinsed it away in the warm water. Grimacing at her reflection, she opened her jar of night cream and massaged it in with firm strokes. That was better. Not so bad for an old lady of sixty-four. Her hair was still shiny, courtesy of Goldwell and her hairdresser. Her figure was excellent thanks to rigorous exercise.

Should she have stayed? No, it wasn't her place. Her heart sped up. But what if there was a '*my place.*' Where would I go?

It flashed in her head. California 1969. The year of the flower children. The year of the moon landing. The year Dave used to talk about with yearning. He had been in Los Angeles in 1969. She'd always been a little bit jealous of that. He seemed to recall that year so fondly. He always had the oddest look in his eyes when he talked about it. Almost as if he was asking her a question.

"Letter," he gasped. *"Scrapbook under our wedding picture. Find it."*

She'd shut that memory of his words away with the rest of that terrible day. She'd never looked for the letter. The scrapbooks were stored with the rest of their memorabilia in the diminutive attic.

Lorena shrugged out of her clothes and into her brushed satin nightgown. The fabric warmed and comforted her. She turned down the covers on the bed, carefully placed the ruffled eyelet pillows on the white brocade chair next to the bed, and gazed around her sanctuary. Everything in it promised peace and safety. From the peach wallpaper patterned in a faint satin stripes, to the mist green sheer curtains, and the cozy white bookshelf filled to overflowing with her favorite books. Her gaze fixed on the framed motto hand lettered. *'I am safe and whole and complete as I am, lacking no one and needing no special something'*

Lorena reached over and took it down. "Bite me." She thrust it under the bed.

She pulled *Eclipse* by Stephanie Meyers from the bookcase, found her place and settled back. Right now she needed to read about people that would love forever. She didn't give a hoot about vampires or werewolves. True love forever . . . that was another matter.

She read till she couldn't focus any longer. She turned out the light and let her thoughts drift. The memory bloomed. *"Say hello to Peter Pan for me."*

Her eyes struggled to open. Oh no, it wasn't possible! Was it? Caught between waking and dreaming, her last thought was *I've got to find that scrapbook.*

Chapter 15
Sherry

Jeremy's face lit up at the sight of her luggage. He took the case from her and dropped it in the living room. "You're staying?" He drew her close and looked down at her. "I'm sorry about this morning. I knew I was behaving like an idiot, but I couldn't stop myself."

Her words rushed out. "Jeremy, I can't promise you forever, no matter how much I want to. I have to go home in two weeks."

"I understand about obligations." His face shadowed. "I've got a few of those myself."

Tell him! She drew a deep breath. Air whooshed out of her lungs.

I can't. She laid her face against his chest. "I need to tell you why," she whispered, "but for a little while, could we pretend we're going to live happily ever after?"

He lifted her chin with a gentle finger. "Here's the thing, Sherry, if there's one lesson I've learned in the last two years, it's that there's no such thing as safe." His lips curved in a smile, but his eyes looked like they'd seen too much sorrow. "I could fall under the wheels of a bus. Some government could unleash that bomb of mine tomorrow. So, yes. Let's take this time and make it our forever."

She reached up to touch his face. Desire rose in a smoky cloud surrounding them.

Jeremy caught her hands and tugged them behind him. His lips took hers in a mind-numbing kiss. Past, present, and future dissolved in the perfection of now. They didn't make it to the bedroom.

After an eternity, Sherry rolled over and sighed. "This carpet is scratchy."

"I don't mind. I can't feel anything but you." He lifted her and settled her body on his. "Is this better?"

"Hmmm," she agreed, snuggling into his warm body. "I guess we can stay right here." The room was cold. It coated her back with shivers.

He rolled her off, stood, and lifted her to her feet. "Have you got a jumper in that suitcase?"

She clung to him. "I don't need it." Her stomach growled. His answered. They broke apart laughing. Both still trembling from the aftershock of loving.

"Let's get you warm. Then I'll feed you." He grabbed her suitcase and took it up the stairs. She gathered up her strewn clothes and followed.

He draped his robe around her and led her into the bathroom. "We'll warm up in the shower. It's big enough for two."

He turned the taps and the water hissed through them in little spurts. "This may take a moment." He folded her into his arms and bent to kiss her. "We can wait."

Clouds of steam filled the room. He slipped the robe off her shoulders and lifted her into the shower. The hot water drops hit her. "Yikes." She stepped backward.

He climbed in, protecting her and adjusted the temperature. Sherry felt small and fragile next to him. If only he could be her forever.

He moved so she could feel the spray. "Is that better?"

"Mmmm." She reveled in the now perfect temperature.

He picked up the soap and ran it down her body in soft caressing strokes.

Her body came alive under his touch. She took the soap from him and returned the favor. Slowly, languidly, she stroked him. He took a cloth and slicked it down her body. Desire sprung up anew. She couldn't get enough of him. She saw a need and urgency in his eyes which matched her own. He lifted her up and slid her onto his shaft, his arms protecting her from the tiled wall as she wrapped her legs around him. Her head tilted back, eyes closed against the streaming water as her body rose and fell in a dance made new. Her world centered on his body moving with her till she arched into an aching wave of pleasure and tumbled into delirium.

Jeremy cradled her in his arms and rested his cheek on her head.

She could feel the thudding of his heart. She ran her fingers between his wet plastered curls. "I've never done that before. It was . . ." The water turned cold. She shrieked.

Jeremy hauled her out of the shower and enveloped them both in a towel.

"My hero." She shook her head and droplets flew across the room. She shivered "What I wouldn't give for a hair dryer."

"Doesn't that enormous case have one?" he teased. He took a smaller towel and wrapped it around her head.

"Nope. Forgot."

"I thought Americans never traveled without their hair dryers."

"You use a different current here. American hair dryers don't work."

She opened the suitcase and unearthed a soft red sweater and jeans. She grabbed fresh underwear and changed swiftly.

He disappeared into his closet and came out dressed in worn jeans and a cream-colored Irish knit sweater.

"That sweater looks warmer than mine."

Jeremy leered. "Ah, but yours fits so nicely."

She smiled up at him and waited.

He went back in the closet and came out holding an almost identical sweater. "My mum gifts me with these at Christmas. She is convinced I cannot look after myself."

Sherry put on the sweater and admired it in the mirror. She picked up her brush to run through her tangled hair.

"No. Let me." He pushed her gently onto the bed and began to draw the brush through her hair in soft caressing strokes.

Sherry shivered with pleasure. "Where did you learn to do that?"

"Two younger sisters," he mumbled.

"Two?" Sherry envisioned another sister invasion.

Courtney's away at school. She won't be banging on the door." He lifted a strand of her hair and inhaled. "Lovely."

Sherry stiffened. "Jen. Rats! Lorena told Jen we'd meet her after rehearsal today."

He buried his face in her hair. "I'm sure they'll manage to have fun without you."

"Lorena went home." Sherry shifted uncomfortably. "She got a call from . . . from her agent." She hated lying, but she couldn't tell him Lorena had an interview with a magazine that didn't exist yet. "She has an audition for a film. It was rather sudden."

Jeremy said nothing.

Sherry relaxed.

He continued the long soothing strokes.

"Hungry?" he asked presently.

"Starved."

Jeremy got another towel from the cupboard in the hall. He draped it around her shoulders. "You shouldn't go out with wet hair. We'll do take out. How do you feel about curry?"

"Love it."

"There's a curry place two blocks from here. I'll go pick some up."

She followed him downstairs.

He put a match to the gas fire. Orange and blue flames flared up wafting warmth and comfort.

"Mmm, lovely." Snuggling into the sofa, she watched him select a bottle of wine from the rack in the dining room.

He expertly uncorked it and grabbed two wine glasses between the fingers of one hand.

"One would almost think you'd done this before," Sherry said with a straight face. "Tell me, Mr. Smythe, exactly how many girls have you seduced in here?"

Jeremy sighed. "I was a wayward youth, once I discovered what girls were for. But that's all over now. He poured her a glass of wine and switched on the TV for her. "Enjoy yourself. I'll be back in a tick."

Sherry stared in fascination at *The Week That Was*. It used to be one of her favorite programs. She listened to David Frost's crisp nasal tones in bemusement.

Jeremy observed her fascination wryly. "Try not to miss me too much."

She waved him out with an absent-minded hand.

By the time he got back, she was watching Fanny Craddock's attempt to liven up the culinary lives of Britons with her strangely hectoring cookery program. Fanny's advice on how to get the better of a fishwife had Sherry giggling uncontrollably.

The cardboard carriers emitted enticing fragrances. "I got Masala curry, rice, and Naan bread. I hope you like them."

"Goody! Let's eat." They went into the kitchen and opened the containers.

Sherry dipped a spoon in the curry. A thread of sweet curled round the spiciness. "This is perfect." She piled her plate with rice and curry and took a slice of the crisp Naan bread.

They took their plates to the living room. *Dr. Who* had replaced Fanny Craddock.

"Do you like this one?" Jeremy asked. "Or shall I switch on some music?"

"No, please. I haven't seen this in such a long time. It's one of my favorites."

Jeremy leaned back and put his free arm around her. "I suppose long is a relative word. I mean it's on every week."

Sherry stopped mid forkful. "I know but . . . I don't watch television often. This is a real treat."

Jeremy divided his attention between his food and watching her.

She looked up and caught his stare. "What? Is there food on my face?"

"No," he said slowly. "I simply can't believe my luck. I can't believe you are here. I like watching you. Did you know you have a little freckle at the corner of your right eye?"

The expression in his eyes stopped her breath. This beautiful man, who'd haunted her memory for so long, loved her. Wordless joy and gratitude welled up inside her. "Watch the TV," she mumbled, suddenly embarrassed.

He obediently looked at the program. When it was over, they gathered up the plates and took them to the kitchen.

"You hunted the food. I'll do the cleanup." She plugged the sink with the stopper and ran it full of soapy water.

Jeremy put the plates in the sink and turned off the water. "Leave them."

He led her back to the living room and put a 33 record on the stereo. "There is something important I need to find out about you." His breath was warm on her cheek. The haunting strains of "Begin the Beguine" filled the air. "Dance with me."

Her arm stole up to his shoulder. His arm dropped to her waist. Their free hands met in a promise. She drifted with him on a cloud of music.

The music stopped. They kept dancing. He pressed her body closer. They fit so perfectly.

Jeremy dropped a butterfly kiss on each eye, his lips soft and warm against her skin. "I knew there was something I needed in this world. I didn't know it was you."

She caught her breath and leaned into him. It was as if each kiss released another bit of knowing.

"Come upstairs," he said softly. "Let me show you."

She nodded. They walked up the stairs twined in each other's arms. This time he left the light off. They didn't need it. They knew each other's scent. The silken velvet touches. The flashes of heat. The spiral of universes as their bodies came together. They fell asleep in each other's arms.

Chapter 16
Lorena

"Lorena! Pick up. It's your agent. Lorena! Pick up! It's your agent," the iPhone blared.

The irritating ring dragged her out of the murky fog of her dream. She groped for the phone, eyes still shut. "Go way," she mumbled. "I'm on break."

"Jesus, Lorena," Brenda snarled. "I hope you were in the shower. This is my third call. You have an interview with *People* at noon."

Lorena glanced at her bedside clock. *Oops.* "I forgot to set the alarm."

"Joyce and I are picking you up at ten forty-five. Get cracking."

Lorena stared at the blank phone screen blearily. No time to look for the letter. It would have to wait until after the interview. No, scratch that. Until after her play date with Dylan. She raced for the shower.

"I want to tell you a secret," Dylan whispered. He pulled Lorena's head down to his level. "I kissed a girl." He pushed her away so he could see her reaction. His brown eyes twinkled up at her.

Lorena looked properly shocked. "Dylan Crawford! You are only four-years-old. You are too young to be doing that."

"It's okay," he said. "I asked her to marry me first. She said yes."

Lorena reached down and caught him up in a hug. "Of course she said yes. Who is the lucky girl?"

Dylan pointed to a little pixie with a straggly blonde ponytail. "Her name is Chelsea, but she is going to change it to Lois Lane."

They followed a line of children and grownups to the next clue in the scavenger hunt. Lorena looked at the papier-mâché rock structure in front of them. "You want me to crawl in there?"

"Uh-huh. C'mon."

Dylan went to a Presbyterian preschool and they were studying superheroes of the Bible. Today it was David. The first adult read the message about how David played the harp and made beautiful songs. They each put a paper harp in their bag and crawled out in search of the next clue.

"It's near the chapel," Chelsea shouted. "That's where the big rock is." Dylan grabbed Lorena's hand and ran after Chelsea.

They finished the afternoon coloring buttons for their superhero capes. Lorena sat on the floor and handed Dylan his crayons.

Claire had to stay until the last child was picked up. "How do you do this?" Lorena wondered. "The noise alone would kill me."

Dylan had run off to play with his fiancée.

Claire folded capes and managed to simultaneously say goodbye to the parents and talk to Lorena. "Don't give me that, Mom. You ran a Girl Scout troop. I would say they made at least this much noise."

"You're right," Lorena conceded. "I had forgotten how loud you all were. Too many years of peace I suppose." She watched Claire put away the children's scrapbooks. "That was a lovely adventure you gave them. I could never organize a scavenger hunt. Too complicated. I don't know how you managed so many trails crossing."

Claire winced. "Me neither. I thought I would go nuts figuring it out, but they had a good time. Are you coming over for dinner?"

Lorena gave an inward sigh as she thought of the scrapbook. "Of course."

Claire cooked spaghetti. Dylan wanted Lorena to play with him in his room. They read books together until dinner was ready.

After dinner, Claire sent Dylan and Jeff off to bath time. She poured herself and Lorena a glass of wine and leaned back on the sofa with a sigh of relief. She turned on her favorite *Dancing with the Stars*. "Thank heavens for DVR. I am only two episodes behind now. Didn't you tell me things would get easier as he got older?"

"Claire, for you I am not sure things will ever get easier. You *look* for things to do. If you're not busy enough, you get involved in something else."

Claire sat up. "Did I tell you I joined a writers group?"

"Where are you going to find time to do that?" Lorena asked.

"Saturday. Saturday Jeff takes charge of Dylan so I have all day to write. Well, all day after Dylan's soccer game. I have to be there for that."

"You're a wonderful writer. I am glad you're finding time for yourself to keep it up."

Lorena left after the show ended, pleading exhaustion. Once home, she went straight to the laundry room, pulled the cord which let down the folding steps, climbed up, and flipped on the attic light switch. The boxes stretched endlessly into the distance.

She hitched her way up onto the floor and crawled toward the back. Standing upright was out of the question. She peered at the labels on the boxes. *Books. Pictures. Claire-Toys. Mother's China.* Why did they have so much stuff? She crawled on. *Claire-Summer Clothes. Claire-Baby clothes.*

Her heart jumped. There it was. *Scrapbooks.* She pushed the box toward the stairs. She moved onto the stairs and realized there was no way she could get the box down by herself. Muttering soft imprecations, she pulled off the tape and opened it.

She pulled out Claire's baby book. Put it aside. She lifted the next book. Claire's high school memories. She took out three more books and finally, there it was. The white puffy plastic book with the words *Our Wedding* on it. She lifted it and slowly backed down the stairs clutching her prize. The dust rising from the book made her sneeze. She got a damp cloth and carefully wiped the cover.

Switching on the reading lamp she snuggled into the sofa and slowly opened the wedding album. She blinked back tears. How young they had been. Her hair was shoulder length and caught back in carefully arranged curls. And Dave. His hair was longer then. His brown glorious eyes were the same, crinkled in laughter.

She turned to the next page. The cake feeding. They were shoving cake into each other's mouth. Lorena remembered she had almost choked on it. It had been a good cake. Her mother had moaned because it wasn't a traditional white cake. They'd chosen instead a decadent chocolate cake frosted in white and covered with garlands of green vines. Dave liked chocolate best. So did she.

David chose the cake topper. Small figurines of Mickey Mouse and Minnie Mouse getting married. Lorena protested because they had never been to Disneyland. He'd smiled a funny little smile and said, "Don't worry, honey, we will. Trust me on this one, okay?"

They went to Los Angeles on their honeymoon. She argued with Dave that they couldn't afford it but he was adamant. He said some things were meant to be and this was one of them. They'd walked on the beach in Santa Monica, and seen the footprints at Grauman's Chinese Theatre. And they'd spent two days in Disneyland. David splurged for a room at the Disneyland hotel.

Lorena turned the page and caught her breath. She had forgotten this picture. An eight-by-ten of them sitting on a wall in her parents' garden. Dave had his arm around her. The light from the sunset shone on their faces. They looked so 'happily ever after' and oh god, they had been.

She touched the picture with one finger. It was sticking out a bit from the page. Something crackled. Carefully, she peeled back the plastic and revealed a sheet of paper covered in Dave's beloved scraggly writing. She lifted it from the book and smoothed it open. The letters danced crazily. She winked back the tears, trying to focus on the page. No use. Wiping her eyes with the back of her hand, she refocused. This time the words made sense. *My darling Lorena if you are reading this and I am not with you, I am dead, which is too bad because I wanted to try it too.*

Lorena blinked. Try what?

I have loved you since the first minute I saw you, nothing will ever change that. Wherever I am right now, I know that I still love you. It isn't possible for us not to be together again. Death is a curtain and I am on the other side. But know this now Lorena, I will be seriously pissed if you try to join me before the appointed time and you know you do not want to see me seriously pissed.

I don't know why I wrote that. I know you too well. You would never do something like that to Claire.

Do you remember the day on Mackinac when I walked up to you and offered you some cotton candy? In our whole life together that has been your first memory of us.

My first memory of us was on July seventh, 1969 at Schwab's Drugstore at 3:00. Close your mouth Lorena. It's true.

In the future, you are going to go to a place called The Castle and somehow, impossibly, improbably, you are going to wind up in the past.

In July of 1969 we had two amazing weeks together. I know this is going to happen because that's when we first met. I am not going to tell you anymore about it. Why should I spoil the surprise? Your future is our past and I will be waiting. Remember. July, 7th, 1969. 3:00 PM. Schwab's drugstore on Sunset Boulevard. I will be the one at the counter who doesn't know you. You will walk up to me and start a conversation about . . .

She turned the page over. There was nothing there. "About *what*?" she shouted. She held the paper up to the light. No writing that had been washed away. Her heart thumped. "About what?" she whispered. Sometimes Dave had the darndest sense of humor. She tried to stop her hands from shaking and read the letter again. Her breath came out in little pants. More time. She was going to have more time with David. She folded the letter carefully and held it to her heart.

Chapter 17
Sherry

"I can't believe Lorena flew off like that." Jen's petulant tone contrasted sharply with the suspicious glances she aimed in Sherry's direction when she thought Jeremy wasn't looking. Jen's high-heeled boots clicked a rhythm on the pavement that sounded like *Guilty. Guilty. Guilty.*

Does Jen think I murdered her? Sherry stepped up her pace trying to keep up with Jen's long legged stride. "You're an actress. I bet you'd go flying off too if someone called you with a great role."

"I wouldn't rush off without leaving a note." Jen sniffed. "I have better manners than that."

"Stuff it, brat." Jeremy put his arm through Jen's companionably. "If you had a chance to read for a film with Robert Redford, you'd be off without a second thought."

Jen stared up at him wide eyed. "Robert Redford? Truly?"

"She didn't say who was in the film," Sherry said, giving Jeremy an admonitory glance. "Your brother's pulling your leg."

"Pig," Jen said without heat. She leaned around Jeremy to glare at Sherry. "Why didn't you go home with her? Don't you have a shop to look after? A boyfriend too, I imagine Americans probably go for that wide eyed Audrey Hepburn look."

Jeremy put a possessive arm around Sherry. "I imagine Sherry's appeal is universal," he said mildly, "but for the moment, she's mine. So get used to it."

Jen subsided.

"Looks like we're first here." Jeremy seated them both at one of the Golden Hind's large oak tables.

"They'll be along soon. That purple makeup is a bear to get off." Jen draped her faux fur over the back of the chair. "They're going to be starving. Go order a huge plate of sausage rolls and piles of chips and a couple of pitchers of Boddingtons."

Jeremy leaned back and folded his arms.

Jen looked surprised. "Oh, come on. You can afford it."

"I believe there was some mention of your excellent manners earlier?"

"Cor! You sound like Mums. All right," she said grudgingly. "*Please.*"

"Much better." Jeremy stood and smiled down at Sherry. "What would you like?"

"Ginger beer, please." She rose. "I'll come with you." " Being left alone at a table with Jen was not a happy thought.

"No, I can manage." The gleam in Jeremy's eyes told her he knew what she was thinking. "You two can have a nice cozy chat."

"*Beast,*" she mouthed. She sat back down and tried to look comfortable.

Jen stared past Sherry's left ear. "So what did you think of the play?"

"You were wonderful," Sherry said, and meant it. "I'm not sure *Titus Andronicus* is ever going to be a popular play, but your Lavinia was completely true and moving."

Jen gave her a real smile. "Yeah, it's got to be the worst of the Shakespeare plays. That's why we staged it with the villains all wearing purple makeup. They're supposed to be aliens from another planet. We thought it would make it more accessible to the audience."

"Doing it as a Space Rock Opera certainly was . . ." Sherry hunted for a tactful word . . . "Compelling." She smiled at Jen. "I loved your ballad. You have a wonderful voice. You could give Janis Joplin a run for the money." "You think so?" Jen's eyes lit up. "I wish Lorena could have seen it. I wanted to show her what real British Shakespeare looks like."

Sherry bit her lip. If only she could remain straight-faced.

Jen's laughter bubbled up. "All right, so it wasn't exactly traditional, but I still say Shakespeare sounds better when it's done by Brits." She hugged Sherry, animosity seemingly forgotten. "Do you want to go shopping tomorrow?" She looked at Sherry's red Halston disparagingly. "Your wardrobe's a bit sedate for someone your age. I'll take you to Biba's."

"There you are my beauty. Thanks for holding the table." John Luterman snagged the chair next to Jen. The rest of the troupe followed, filling up the remaining chairs. John gave Jen a casual kiss and turned to Sherry. "So what did you think of the play?"

"It was quite a show." Jeremy placed two pitchers of Boddingtons on the table and dropped into the chair next to Sherry. "When do you go on tour?"

The waiter set a tray of glasses and a plate of sausage rolls on the table and went back for more.

"We're booked in Sidmouth on Friday, then on to Birmingham where we'll open *Streetcar*," John replied. He took a sausage roll and bit into it. "So where's Lorena?"

"She flew back to America for a film audition with Robert Redford." Jen looked like Lorena had stolen her lollipop.

"Smashing. What's the name of the film?"

"*Dead Man's Run*," Jeremy said easily. He took possession of Sherry's hand under the table and crossed two of her fingers. He lifted them to his lips and kissed them. "For luck," he whispered, his smile a bit crooked.

Sherry's stomach dropped, He knew she'd lied. Why hadn't he called her on it?

Sherry waited until Jeremy started the car. "Robert Redford? *Dead Man's Run?*"

"Do you know your shoulders tense up when you lie?" Jeremy downshifted and pulled out into traffic.

"I was telling the truth," she protested. "Lorena did go home." Sherry felt her shoulders tense and forced them to relax. I'm not lying. I'm omitting. How can I tell him she walked through a door into the future? "I made up the part about the audition," she confessed, "because I thought it sounded like a polite excuse to leave."

"I thought that might be it," Jeremy said. "I simply added a few details. If you're going to lie, make it a good one. It's more fun that way."

Sherry nodded and leaned back with a sigh. How on earth was she going to tell him the truth in a way that wouldn't sound like science fiction?

Chapter 18
Lorena

She wanted to go tonight. An unbearable rush of excitement clouded her senses.

"Calm down, Lorena. You can't just disappear." Her fingers tapped a staccato on the scrapbook. What kind of an excuse could she come up with to be out of touch for two weeks?

A line from the last episode of *Looking for Love* flashed in her mind. *When in doubt, retreat.* Yes! She powered up her computer and Googled spa retreats.

The Expanding Light in Nevada City, California was far enough away so Claire wouldn't drive up for a visit. She lit a cigarette and composed an email to Brenda and her publicist to book out for two weeks for a Spa retreat. A wave of exhaustion rolled over her. Must be the time travelling . . . or the time difference . . . "Got to sleep." She yawned. "I'll call Claire tomorrow."

The phone woke her. She had fallen asleep with *Eclipse* under her cheek. She gingerly rubbed the imprint on her face

"'Lo," she mumbled blearily.

"Mom, can you do me a favor and babysit Dylan tonight?"

That cleared the sleep from her head. "Oh, honey, I am so sorry, but Sherry called me last night and we are leaving for a retreat this afternoon."

"Wow! You didn't say anything about it yesterday."

"I didn't know yesterday. We were on a waiting list and got lucky."

"Where are you going?"

"*The Expanding Light*. It's in Nevada City up past Sacramento." She could hear the click of Claire's computer keys. Claire loved to Google. Thank god she'd picked a real place.

"Look's beautiful. How long will you be gone?"

"Two weeks. It's going to be wonderful. They have yoga and inner silence meditation and Ayurvedic treatments."

"O–kay . . . Call me when you get there."

Lorena hated Claire's 'Mom, what are you doing now?' voice. "No. I can't get phone calls. That's part of the retreat. We leave the outer world for two weeks."

There was silence on Claire's end of the phone.

Lorena rushed to fill it. "I love you very much. Kiss Dylan for me."

"Mom, are you all right?"

"Never better, dear." She was going to see Dave. Nothing was better than that. "I'll call you when I get back. I am sure it will be a whole new me." She made kissing noises and hung up.

Her wedding ring flashed in the morning sunlight. "Damn. I can't show up to meet Dave wearing a wedding ring." Lorena ran her fingers lovingly over the five pearls surrounded by chip diamonds and slowly drew it off her finger. The white ring of skin seemed like a betrayal. Her lips firmed. "Suck it up, Lorena. You'll put it on when you get back." She put the wedding ring in her jewelry box and dashed for the shower. She needed to be out of here before her concerned daughter hunted her down.

The Brad Pitt Maître d' was off duty. This one looked like a young Steve Martin. He eyed Lorena's pink mini dress and kitten heels and ushered her to the *Choose your Adventure* door.

Lorena's heartbeat accelerated in tempo with the computer thrumming. Had she forgotten anything? She'd gone to Sherry's, re-recorded Sherry's greeting, and penned a note. *Sherry, check your machine. I told Claire we were going to the Expanding Light Spa in Nevada City. I am off to The Castle to try 1969 Los Angeles. I'll see you when I get back.*

Next she'd raided Sherry's closet and transferred her clothes and makeup into a huge woven purse that looked like it was born in the sixties. Much easier to handle than a heavy suitcase. She'd called her agent from her cell and used traffic as an excuse to cut off Brenda's loud complaints.

Lorena ticked off her mental list and took a calming breath. She shifted the heavy bag to her left shoulder and walked to the desk, masking her nerves with a sunny smile.

The girl behind the computer had purple streaked hair and a nametag that read *Trish*. Her cropped black T-shirt exposed two silver rings piercing her navel.

Trish looked up and removed her earplugs. "Hi!" Her voice didn't match her appearance. She sounded like Mae West. "Where would you like to go?"

"Los Angeles, in July of 1969. Can you get me there?"

The girl nodded approvingly at Lorena's mini dress. "You've done your homework. Any particular date?"

"July seventh, please."

"May I see your credit card and driver's license, please? Lorena handed them over. Trish studied Lorena's driver's license. She looked up and smiled. "I'm a big fan. Ms. Anderson. I love your work." She hesitated, then blurted out. "I have to ask you this. Have you any strong memories of that place? Because that can cause some problems with the program."

"I wasn't anywhere near Los Angeles in 1969. I'm doing some research for an upcoming role." Well, the first part was true.

Trish looked relieved. "That's okay then." She tapped briskly on the keyboard. "How long do you think your research will take?"

"I'm not sure." Lorena gave Trish her best sincere smile. "I want to get a feel for Los Angeles in that time period."

"A ticket is good for two weeks. I hope you find everything you need there."

"So do I." Her heart thumped so loudly she was afraid Trish would hear it.

Trish handed her back her card, a ticket, and book of traveler's checks. "Hall to my right. Follow the peace signs. Enjoy yourself."

Lorena stuffed the card back in her purse and walked through the door to the hall.

The dancing peace signs led her along the corridor to the music of The 5th Dimension. Lorena took a deep breath and slid the ticket into the slot. Closing the door behind her, she shut her eyes and waited for the blue light. The mild electric tingle traveled down her body. Her stomach churned at the floor's dropping sensation. When it stopped, she opened the second door.

She was on the corner of Hollywood and Vine. Across the street was the substantial Broadway department store. On the left side of Hollywood Boulevard was a coffee shop called Aldo's. Lorena winced at the heat coming up from the pavement.

Three hippies, two girls and a boy, were singing "Age of Aquarius" and banging tambourines. Their long tangled hair could have used a good shampooing. Further down the street, she could see more teenagers lounging in doorways, panhandling the people passing by. Lorena was reasonably sure that whatever they were smoking wasn't legal.

There was the usual complement of tourist types. That hadn't changed. The street still glittered with tiny sparkles. Lorena always thought the streets of Hollywood looked like they were paved with gold. She looked down at the sidewalk and drew a startled breath. The square plaque with the center circle containing the names Neil Armstrong, Buzz Aldrin, Michael Collins, and Apollo XI wasn't there.

She crossed the boulevard and walked to the newsstand below Hollywood on Cahuenga. The headline on the Herald Examiner read **US Begins Troop Withdrawals.** She checked the date on the corner of the paper. July 7, 1969.

Horns honked. People strolled at a desultory pace. Lorena reached up and felt her face. Smooth. Soft. Unlined. She retraced her steps to The Broadway and made her way to the third floor women's restroom. Her reflection smiled back at her in the elegant mirror. Honey streaked hair waved below her shoulders. Her eyes were wide and bare of makeup.

Pulling out her makeup kit, she swiftly did her face. Heavy on the black eyeliner, light on the lipstick. She expertly attached the furry eyelashes. Okay, a little much, but she didn't care. She felt beautiful

Lorena made her way downstairs and back to the street. She'd take a bus, she decided. The sign on the theater opposite the Brown Derby read **David Frost Live. Guests tonight Tommy Steele and Rep. Adam Clayton Powell.** Lorena grinned. She'd had a huge crush on Tommy Steele when he played in the musical *Half a Sixpence* on Broadway. He was the kind of blue-eyed blond she used to be attracted to before she met Dave.

A crowd of people waited for the bus. She glanced at her watch. 1:30. She had time.

"I don't believe it's real. I think it's another Hollywood stunt." The nasal voice came from a bald headed man with a Hawaiian shirt and a camera around his neck. He was sweating heavily.

"Can it, Rupert," his companion replied.

She had to be his wife, Lorena decided, her dress matched his shirt.

The woman pulled out a pack of Tareytons and lit up. "In two weeks we are going to land a rocket on the moon. Why would Hollywood go to all that trouble? To make people watch more TV?"

Lorena smiled. Of course. July was the month man first set foot on the moon. She savored the words in her mind *One small step for man* . . . The bus lumbered to a halt. Lorena watched carefully to see how much money the person ahead of her dropped in the machine. Twenty-five cents. Amazing. She dropped in a quarter and moved to the left hand side. She knew approximately where Schwab's was. Near the corner of La Cienega and Sunset. About where the House of Blues would be in the future.

With a roar of exhaust the bus lumbered forward. She regarded the scene with fascination, trying to orient it with the overlay in her mind of what Hollywood looked like yesterday when she'd been interviewed by *People* at Musso and Frank's. The surrounding buildings were different, but Musso and Frank hadn't changed a bit. Still the same staid sign. Probably the same grim faced waiters. The bus turned down Highland Avenue and right onto Sunset Boulevard. Hollywood High School looked the same. Other buildings were unfamiliar. They passed the Mayfair market, Fairfax Avenue.

As the strip got closer her breathing grew rapid. They passed the giant Bullwinkle statue. Lorena tensed when she saw the sign *Schwab's Pharmacy* in scripted letters. Reaching up, she yanked the cord. The rear door sighed open. Lorena waved a thank-you to the driver and stepped down.

The air felt like a sauna compared to the coolness of the bus. The bus blew a blast of exhaust. She crinkled her nose. Her heart thumped too loudly. She was early. Maybe Dave wasn't here yet. She focused on the façade of the building as she waited for the interminable light to change.

The upper and lower windows of Schwab's Pharmacy gave it a vaguely European look that put it out of step with its more mundane neighbors. A tourist posed for a snapshot in front of the doorway, her hand pointing up at the Schwab's sign. In the forties and fifties, Schwab's had been a hangout for movie stars. James Dean hung out there. Lana Turner had supposedly been discovered sipping a coke at the soda fountain.

When she opened the door, a blast of cool air rushed past her. She scanned the faces of the actors perusing the trade papers in front of the magazine rack. None of them looked familiar. Maybe they'd never made it to famous.

She walked to the makeup section, afraid to look at the soda fountain counter. The noise was a light buzz. She studied the Elizabeth Arden display. They had perfumes. There was Blue Grass, one of her mother's favorites.

What if he isn't here? Lorena lifted her chin. Only one way to find out. She turned around and moved toward the soda fountain.

Chapter 19
Sherry

"How do you feel about hoaxes?"

Sherry almost dropped the teapot. "What kind of hoaxes?"

"Fun ones." Jeremy put his arms around her and reached behind her for a muffin.

She relaxed. "I might have friendly feelings toward them."

He handed her a proof for the next edition of *Twenty-Eight*. The headline was **Spaghetti Harvest in Ticino, Switzerland.**

"You think anyone is going to believe this?" She stared incredulously at the picture of an old man and a nubile young woman plucking strips of pasta off trees."

"Absolutely. The BBC ran a news story on it about ten years ago as an April Fool's joke. Something that good deserves repeating." Jeremy grinned. "They got a lot of calls asking where one could buy a spaghetti tree. They told the callers to place a sprig of spaghetti in a tin of tomato sauce and hope for the best."

Sherry laughed. "You're an absolute zany, and I love you."

She loved everything these days. She'd forgotten what being in love did to your worldview. Her world was new penny bright, full of laughter and smiles.

While Jeremy was at the office, she toured London.

One whole day was consumed by The British Library and its manuscript collection. Sherry paid homage to the glass covered Magna Carta and mooned over hand drawn medieval manuscripts, their colors still untouched by time. The parchment itself had yellowed, but the brilliant scarlets, blues, and golds defied time. She'd browsed the gift shop looking for postcards of the books. The postcards were available, but the colors were not the same. Modern inks couldn't duplicate the richness of the originals. She bought Jeremy a little wooden Beefeater guard figure that amused her.

Jeremy retaliated with bizarre facts about the Tower of London. She hadn't known that Tower once housed a menagerie which included a polar bear, or that Rudolph Hess, Hitler's secretary, was the Tower's last prisoner in 1941.

The day before Sherry had gone shopping with Jen for costumes and discovered Trinity Church Hospice on Kensington Road. It was a treasure trove of clothing from the 1930's. She bought a suitcase full of camisoles, teddies, negligees, and satin evening dresses to take home for the shop. They served to remind her that *Now and Then* existed. It was so easy to stay in the present moment.

"Whither shall you wander today, my love?"

"I'm going bargain hunting at Oxfam."

Jeremy shuddered. "Better you than me, although," he reflected. "I quite liked that negligee thingy you modeled last night."

"I would never have guessed. You got it off me so quickly I thought it was hurting your eyes."

Jeremy put on his jacket. "Be home early, love. I thought we would dine with Sherlock Holmes tonight."

"Another hoax?"

"Perish the thought. I would never hoax you." He drew her up and lifted her chin for a kiss. "I love you too much for that."

She bent her head and gazed at his top button. Now.

She'd already waited too long Now, before he hates me. "Jeremy," she began.

"Hold that thought, love. I'm late again." He started out the door. "You'll love Simpson's," he called over his shoulder. "Sherlock and Watson used to dine there after one of their cases. That's why I said we'd be dining with them." The door closed behind him.

Another reprieve. She dropped back in her seat. Telling him felt like it might be a death sentence and she didn't want to lose what they shared.

"You're a coward," she accused herself.

Sherry picked up the dishes and dumped them in the sink. "Damn right," she answered back. "Just a few more days . . ."

Oxfam proved a disappointment. "You've come too late in the day, love" the sales clerk advised her. "You need to come round about seven in the morning. We've got some dedicated shoppers here. They always skim the cream."

"I'm looking for clothes from the twenties and thirties. Any suggestions?" Sherry asked.

"You might trot 'round to St. Ethelred's charity shop. It's two blocks further, behind St. Ethelred's church. I got a beautiful handbag there last week. It looked like something that might have belonged to the Queen Mum." The clerk leaned over and whispered to Sherry, "I've heard they get some of their stock from the palace."

"Thanks." Sherry smiled. "I'll do that." She handed over the red and gold bound books she'd picked up. "I'll take these."

The clerk read the titles. "*Lord of the Rings,* eh? My son Trevor loves those books. He's always going on about them."

Sherry laughed. "My oldest son is the same way. He's a Tolkien fanatic."

The clerk looked at her strangely. "You look a bit young

to have a son who'd be interested in these books. Is he some kind of genius?"

Sherry flushed. Being sixty-three in a twenty-year-old-body had its pitfalls. "I meant my sister's oldest son. Didn't I say that?" She rushed on, "John is thirty-two. My sister is much older than I am." She paid for her purchases and left quickly.

She stopped at the Lyons Corner House on the next block and ordered a pot of tea and some scones. She sat at a wood café table and opened *The Lord of the Rings*. The publication date was 1966. It didn't look like a first edition, but she was sure John would love it. John was a Tolkien Groupie. He'd met his wife Janie at a midnight screening of *Lord of The Rings*.

Sherry put the book away and concentrated on the scones. She was always hungry these days and everything tasted wonderful. She eyed the steak and kidney pies and the Eccles' cake in the glass counter. Jeremy would love them. She'd take some home.

Home. It was beginning to feel that way. Her real life felt more distant every day. Sherry opened her wallet to the only picture she carried of John and Michael. They smiled back at her. Michael wearing his graduation cap and gown proudly and John making rabbit ears behind Michael's head. She took the picture out and caressed its glossy surface with soft fingers. Her beautiful, funny, grown up boys.

She needed to get a souvenir for Michael too. What about that museum Jeremy mentioned in his quest to acquaint her with the more bizarre haunts of London? The Old Operating Theatre. He said it was in the garret of a church and that students used to go there to watch operations in the days before anesthesia. She'd denied any interest in seeing it, but the gift shop would probably have the perfect memento for a third year medical student.

Sherry blinked. Were John and Michael getting a little

blurry? *Her heart pounded.* She had a sudden terrifying flashback to the movie *Back to the Future* when Michael Fox and his brother and sister began to disappear from the picture because he'd changed the future.

She blinked again and a tear fell on the picture, smearing Michael's face. Grabbing a napkin, Sherry carefully blotted it away. The picture was clear again except the tearstain on Michaels's eyes. The moment of fright stayed with her until evening when the feel of Jeremy's arms around her and his lips on hers sent it scurrying to the back of her mind.

Jeremy rolled over and looked at her as if he was memorizing her face. He wove her hair through his fingers, stroking and loving. Sherry snuggled closer playing with his chest, covering it with tiny kisses, savoring his scent.

"What do you know about cricket?" he asked out of nowhere.

"The game or the insect?"

"The game."

"I don't understand it. I've read lots of books about it. When I lived here, I raided Harrods children's bookshelves and cricket was mentioned in a lot of the boarding school books. I even read PG Wodehouse's book that had cricket in it."

"PG Wodehouse wrote about cricket?"

"Yes, I don't remember the name of the book, but I didn't get the game. It doesn't make sense to me. Only the English could come up with something that weird."

"It's very simple," Jeremy said kindly. "It's a lot like baseball."

"It can't be. I understand baseball. And a baseball game doesn't take place over several days. I have heard of cricket matches that ran that long."

"No, really," he insisted. "You have two teams of eleven

players each and they have to score runs. The game starts with a coin toss. Here I'll show you."

He reached into the bedside table drawer and pulled out a pad and a pencil and started diagramming. "All eleven players of the fielding team go out to field. Two players of the batting team go out to bat."

Sherry could feel her eyes begin to glaze over.

Jeremy dropped a kiss on her head. "Pay close attention. There may be a quiz afterward." He went back to his diagramming. "The fielding team wants to stop the batters from making any runs. See," he beamed, "it's like baseball. One fielder is the bowler. He takes the ball. Another fielder is the wicket keeper. He squats behind the opposite wicket."

Sherry covered the diagram with her hand. "Okay, why are we talking about cricket?"

"Well, there is a game this Saturday, and I thought you might like to go. My team is playing."

"Your team? You play cricket?"

Jeremy nodded. "Come on," he pleaded. "You're in England. This is something you should see."

Sherry sighed. She couldn't resist the hopeful look on his face. "I don't suppose you'd rather go to the theatre?"

Jeremy brightened. "We could do both. The National Theatre Company is doing Zefferelli's version of *Much Ado About Nothing*. We could see that tomorrow night."

"The National Theatre Company? Yes! I would love it." Sherry stroked his shoulder reveling in the smooth play of muscle under velvet skin. "Are you sure you're ready for more Shakespeare?" she teased. "I wasn't sure you were going to survive *Titus Andronicus*."

"It was a close run thing. I'm glad they've gone on tour. I don't think I could stand another performance of that play." His eyes twinkled. "I'll have you know Jen isn't the only actor in the family. I played Lady Macbeth when I was in the fifth form."

She tried to visualize it and gave up with a giggle. "That I would love to have seen." Her fingers skimmed his beard-roughened cheek. "Were you a very pretty boy?"

Jeremy looked revolted. "No. I had chipped knees and freckles. Boys are never pretty."

Sherry smoothed away his frown. "You had to have been very handsome. Look at you now." She dropped a kiss on the end of his nose. "Do you have any pictures?"

"No. My Mum does. She is an obsessive collector. The house is filled with scrapbooks of all four of us. She was determined to document every phase of our existence."

"I would love to meet your mother."

"That could be arranged."

Sherry withdrew. Since she couldn't stay, the fewer connections she made the better.

"You look sad. What's wrong?"

"Nothing." She pasted a smile on her face. "A goose walked over my grave."

"It's my family," he said straight faced. "When I think of them, I often get that same feeling."

Sherry pushed him down on the bed and straddled him. "So when do I get to see where you work?"

Jeremy pulled her head down to his shoulder. "It's not very posh. A very ordinary office."

"I loved *Queen Victoria reincarnated as Mouse*, but *Aliens in Whitehall* may be your masterpiece.*" She tickled the back of his neck. "Where do you get all this stuff?"

"They come out of the woodwork. It's amazing how much people are willing to believe." He rolled over to look at her. "I know it's not real journalism but it has a certain charm. And people need this stuff. It cannot all be Vietnam and postal strikes and starving babies in Africa. What I do serves its purpose."

Sherry curled a lock of his hair around her finger. "I

wasn't putting you down. And anyway," she quoted, "*There are more things in heaven and earth, than are dreamt of in your philosophy.*'"

Jeremy nodded. "Hamlet."

"Yes." She shifted her body and stared at the window. The rain chased tiny beads down the pane. "Soon I am going to tell you a story worthy of your magazine."

He looked intrigued. "Why not now?"

"Because." Sherry rolled over on top of him. "I have better things to do. I have thought of a very good game. Let's play Vampire and Victim and guess who you get to be?"

Jerry flipped her off and pinned her wrists above her head. "Vampire," he growled. "And if you are very, very good, we'll switch roles next time."

He nuzzled her neck, nipping her with tiny teasing kisses.

"I'm not sure this is a good game after all." Her hands itched to be free so that she could join in the fun. She struggled, but her hands remained pinned.

"Quiet, wench. The Vampire is feeding." The teasing line of kisses, the warm tickling of his breath dropped lower.

All she wanted to do was feel. The warm sensations flickered inside her like tiny lightning bolts feeding the cravings. Her center ignited. Her hands moved restlessly under his restraining grasp.

Her body arched inviting him inside. The teasing slow kisses grew swifter warmer and more intense. Soon he could no longer resist the invitation. He buried himself inside her. She held him in tightly. He was her prisoner now. He began to move slowly at first, then with more and more urgency. She tore her hands free of his grasp and fisted them in his hair. Their lips met in a searing heart-stopping kiss. She forgot to breathe. She spiraled over the edge and into nirvana.

Jeremy collapsed, his head resting across her breasts.

With a limp almost boneless hand she stroked his back.

"I can never get enough of you." He eased himself off, placing her hand on his chest. "You are my own personal miracle."

Sherry's hand drew in the warmth of him. "You are everything I ever dreamed of," she whispered. Her heart felt like a stone in her chest. She'd be leaving soon. A parade of endless days without Jeremy scrolled in her mind.

Jeremy's breath evened, smoothed out into sleep.

The rain stopped. Sherry lay awake staring out the window at the flickered lamp lit patterns left by trees branches moving in the wind.

His arm snaked out and cradled her body. She nestled in willingly. She studied Jeremy lying so peacefully, his breathing deep and even. *Would he marry and father a child.* The thought burned deep and painfully within her. She couldn't ask him not to. He deserved the joys and pains of fatherhood. The joys were so much greater.

"Sherry," he murmured in his sleep.

She eased out of his embrace and groped her way to the bathroom. In her mind, Sherry could see Jeremy with ginger haired sons and daughters and an unnamed faceless blur of a wife. She hated her.

"You're being a bitch," she whispered. "He deserves every bit of happiness he can have in this world." Her throat ached with suppressed tears. "I know that, but I want to be the one to give it to him." She curled up on the floor and sobbed her grief into a towel.

Chapter 20
Lorena

Dave sat at the soda fountain, head bent over a book. His hair was longer, and he wore a black T-shirt, jeans, and sandals. He reached out a long arm and grabbed for his soda. He took a sip from the straw without ever looking up from the book.

The blood rushed to Lorena's head. She grabbed the edge of the counter for support. The only thing she heard was the beating of her own heart. He was here and she was going to be with him again for the first time.

"Now," she whispered. Lorena drifted over to him. She tried to peer over his shoulder to see what he was reading, but couldn't decipher it. She gathered her courage and slipped onto the adjoining stool. He didn't look up. She picked up the menu and studied it unseeingly. What should she say?

"Ready to order?" The freckled faced kid, with a white soda jerk cap tipped to one side, grinned at her.

"Umm," she glanced at Dave's half-empty glass, "I'll have one of those."

"Chocolate ice cream soda? Good choice. You want the whipped cream?"

Lorena nodded. She snuck another look at Dave. She had no idea what to do next. Where's an opening line when I need one?

Dave turned a page and she caught a glimpse of the title. *Stranger in a Strange Land.* Yes! She tapped Dave's arm gently. "I've read that twice. It's wonderful, isn't it?"

Dave looked up. "I'm sorry. What did you say?"

Lorena leaned closer and read over his shoulder. He was at the part when Michael met Jubal Harshaw. "I love that scene. I loved Jubal the minute he was introduced."

Dave gave her a conspiratorial smile. "This is the third time I've read it." He looked her over and seemed to like what he saw. "So, you grok, Heinlein?"

Her heart melted. She breathed in his scent. Old Spice and an indefinable something that was Dave. It was like nectar to her. She cleared her throat. "I do grok." Her voice was husky. She wished there was a glass of water nearby.

"I'm David Cramer and you are . . .?" He put out his hand.

She curled her hand into his. A funny look came over his face, like he'd just been shocked.

"Lorena," she said. "Lorena Anderson."

He continued to hold her hand. Their eyes held each other's. Neither looked away.

"That'll be a dollar, seventy-five." The boy put a cherry-topped whipped cream confection in front of Lorena.

Lorena blinked, took back her hand and fished in her purse for two dollars. "Thank you."

He took the money and turned away.

"No, wait. Could I please have a glass of water?"

"Sure." The boy brought her a small glass of water with no ice. She wrapped her shaking hands around it and took a sip.

Lorena handed Dave the glass and recited the ritual phrase from *Stranger in a Strange Land* whereby two people become one. "May I offer you water?"

Dave reached out and took the glass from her. His eyebrows lifted questioningly.

Lorena knew what he was thinking. She smiled a little tremulously. She nodded and held her breath.

Dave slowly raised the glass to his lips, his eyes never leaving hers. He took a sip and handed it back to her. His hand covered hers as she took the glass. "May you never thirst."

He reached over, brushed a lock of hair back behind her ear, and whispered, "I have never done that before. You had better mean it."

Lorena touched the side of his mouth where there was a drop of wetness. She dried it with her finger. "I do." The moment felt overwhelming.

To break the tension she leaned over the counter and took a sip of her soda. The chocolate bubbles cooled her throat, a delicious accompaniment to the bubbles of joy inside her.

Dave closed the book. "So, Lorena Anderson, who are you? What are you doing here?" His grin had a familiar lopsided tilt. "I want to know a little bit about my water brother?"

"I am here to meet you."

His smile slipped. He looked puzzled and a little wary.

"Forget I said that. I am studying to be an actress. I came to Hollywood to get discovered."

Dave's smile disappeared. His eyes frosted. "An actress. I should have known." He got up and grabbed his book. "Congratulations on a scene well played. Good luck in the movies." He turned away and started out the door.

"No. Wait. Please!" She scrambled for her dropped purse. He didn't break his stride.

She caught him at the door. "Please, listen. I didn't come to Hollywood to get discovered. I lied because you would never believe the truth." She clutched his hand with all her strength. "Please, don't go." Her breath came in little gasps as tears overflowed.

Dave freed his hand and pulled out a handkerchief. He reached down and dabbed at her face. He showed her the black streaks. "A real actress would use waterproof mascara."

"Sorry. As a rule, I'm not a crier, but . . ." Lorena's breath hitched. She took the handkerchief from him and finished wiping her face.

Dave tucked an arm around her and led her out to the street. "Okay, Water Brother, where's your car?"

"I don't have one."

He gave her the *look* all Angelenos give the carless. "All right. I'll give you a lift home. Where do you live?"

Lorena tried to think of a plausible answer and failed. Her shoulders drooped. "Nowhere at the moment." She looked up at him. "I'm kind of out of answers right now. I'm afraid to lie again. Could we go to your place?"

Dave's body stiffened. "I suppose you already know where that is?"

"No, I don't. You never talked about this much."

Dave stared at her, his brows furrowed. "Have we met before? I can't imagine forgetting you."

Lorena wanted to scream. "Damn this is so complicated," she whispered through stiff lips. "I don't know what to do."

Dave looked down into her tear-filled eyes and sighed resignedly. "We'll go to my place. Come on. My car's parked around the corner."

Lorena leaned into him in sudden relief. "Thank you." She put a hand on his chest. She could feel his heart. What a wonderful sound. *Home.*

Dave's arms tightened around her. He lifted her chin and fitted his lips over hers. Time stopped. The touch of his lips was so familiar and yet so new.

He broke the kiss. His eyes wide with shock. "What was that?" he whispered.

She nestled her head against his chest and sent up a wordless prayer of thankfulness.

A horn honked. A tambourine banged. A rough voice whined, "Can you spare some change, please?"

Dave took a handful of change and threw it in the Hare Krishna's tambourine. He towed Lorena down the street and around the corner and stopped at a beige Volkswagen. He unlocked the door and helped her inside.

"Ouch." The plastic burned her thighs. She jumped out of the car.

"Sorry," Dave said. "I don't usually have a passenger." He looked around the car for something to cover the seat and grabbed a day old newspaper from the back. "Here. Sit on this."

She sat on **Braves Demolish Dodgers 5-2**. It helped. She reached for her seat belt. There wasn't one. She had forgotten there was a time before seat belts. It seemed a little dangerous. "Drive carefully."

Chapter 21
Sherry

Thursday night, they went to dinner before the play with two of Jeremy's friends.

Edward and Susan were obviously in the first stages of love, but that didn't prevent them from quizzing Sherry mercilessly.

"So, where did you meet?" Susan asked, her eyes checking every detail of Sherry's appearance.

Sherry and Jeremy exchanged a quick glance. They chorused "On the tube"—"In a pub."

Edward lifted an eyebrow. "I wasn't aware of a tube that had a pub," he observed dryly.

Susan looked fascinated. "Where is this pub tube?"

Sherry's eyes begged Jeremy to answer for them.

"I first met Sherry a few months ago. We got to chatting and I asked her for her number, but she . . . Ah—I . . . lost it."

Sherry rushed to take up the story. "Yes. I expected him to call but he didn't. So I thought that was the end. Last week I met him again in Shakespeare's and decided to chase the adventure."

Jeremy smiled at her warmly. "I didn't run very fast." He clasped her hand under the table. His forefinger made tiny circles on her wrist.

Sherry took a sip of her ginger beer hoping that they wouldn't notice the warm color in her face. "What about you? How did you two meet?"

Susan giggled. "I ran into him. Literally. I was driving down Kings Cross and he stepped out in front of me. I almost died of fright."

"Were you hurt?" Sherry asked.

Edward regarded his beer. "Only in the region of my heart." He gave Susan an intimate smile and turned back to Jeremy and Sherry. "I stepped out into the street and I felt this push and pain on my leg and a huge squeal of brakes. Susan jumped out of the car screaming, 'I didn't mean it. I am so sorry.'" I got up off the street ready to give her the tongue lashing of her life, and then I saw her."

Susan chimed in. "He didn't say anything at first. I couldn't see him clearly. I was terrified and crying. I had never hit anything before, not even a curb."

"She was crying so hard I didn't think she could stop," Edward continued. "We were attracting a lot of attention so I led her back to the car and put her in the passenger seat. I took her keys, drove the car over to St. Pancras station and parked."

"I finally stopped crying but I was still scared," Susan said. "I mean here was this perfect stranger driving off with me. I thought he might be taking me to the police or to his lair."

"I would have been scared out of my mind," Sherry said. "What did you do?"

"I finally wiped my eyes and looked at him." Susan smiled at Edward. "He was the most beautiful man I had ever seen."

Sherry looked at Edward's rather ordinary face. His dark brown eyes were hidden behind horn-rimmed glasses and his nose was a beak. His short black hair was a bit thin on top. She tried looking at him through Susan's eyes, but she couldn't.

She looked over at Jeremy's dazzling face and wondered if love was the beautifier. Would he still look like

Michelangelo's David if she didn't love him? She rather thought he would. Jeremy's hand played with her leg. She was glad of the long tablecloth and the candle light. Her breathing quickened.

"But what did he say?" Sherry asked Susan. "What did you say?"

"He said that if he was out of his cricket match that weekend, I was going to have to explain it." Susan grinned at Edward and shook her head. "I had nearly killed him and he was talking about cricket."

"Well I wanted to get her mind off the accident," Edward said. "I needed to calm her down so I could get her stats. I knew I didn't want to let her out of my life."

"So I apologized again and he gave me his name and asked if he could buy me a cup of tea." Susan's freckled face shone. "I mean, he must have been in the most tremendous pain but he asked if he could buy me a cup of tea."

"I took her to the Lyons corner house. That may have been the longest tea on record. I never did get back to work. I had a lot of explaining to do the next day."

"So did I. My mum wanted to take away the car, she was that worried. Mum and I work at *The Curling Iron*," Susan said. "But then she met Edward. She's not altogether happy. I never dated much before Edward. She thinks I should see a bit more of life. Edward thinks I should too." She shot a mutinous glance at Edward. "But I am eighteen and old enough to know what I want."

Edward's lips curved. "When I am sure of that, things will be different." He turned the conversation back to Sherry. "So are you going to the game?"

Susan looked at Sherry. "You had better like cricket or your personal match is off."

"Oh, I am willing to like it. I am not sure I understand it."

Jeremy and Edward launched in to a long tangled explanation involving rounders, innings, wickets, and great test matches.

Sherry tuned them out.

Susan leaned over. "What are you wearing then?"

Sherry shrugged. "I don't know. What does one wear to a cricket match?"

"Your very best."

Sherry's eyes widened. "It's a sport. Who gets dressed up for a sport?"

Susan giggled. "We do. Cricket is kind of like a fancy lawn party so people dress up a lot. Sometimes it looks like an opening day at Wimbledon."

"Big hats and pearls?" Sherry asked.

"Well, not pearls," Susan said. "You will certainly want some kind of a hat with a brim. You don't want to get sunburned. And heels. No tennies."

"I've got the heels but I sure don't have the hat."

Susan brightened. "Want to go shopping after work tomorrow? I know a wonderful place on Sidney Street in Chelsea."

Sherry nodded. She didn't want to look wrong in front of Jeremy's friends. "Thanks."

Susan turned to Edward. "Edward, Sherry and I need to go shopping tomorrow."

Jeremy and Edward groaned in unison.

Susan looked at them reproachfully. "Don't rain on our parade. No one is asking you to come. We'll meet you after and we can catch a flick. *Georgy Girl* is on at the Odeon."

"Early night," Edward reminded her. "Match the next day. We'll meet you at a pub. Where are you going?"

"Sidney Street. Right off Kings Road."

Edward nodded. "The Royal Oak is on King's Road two blocks North of Sidney. We can meet up there around eight."

"Seven," Jeremy firmly said. "Keep it short."

"Good idea," Sherry said. "We want them both to be all fresh and daisy-like for the match." Her hand covered Jeremy's knee. His hand covered hers. Her breath shortened. She stopped thinking about the match.

Edward glanced at his watch. "We'd better be moving on. We don't want to miss curtain."

"How did you get the tickets?" Jeremy asked Edward as he pulled out Sherry's chair for her. "A box, no less."

"No partial views for me." Edward grinned, helping Susan on with her coat. His hand lingered on her shoulders. Susan's head tipped back to caress his arm. "My brother Alec knows a chap in the ticket office. Alec knows the darndest people. It's very convenient sometimes."

"Yeah," Jeremy said. "Remember that Welsh wrestler? What was his name? Dai something?"

"Dai Gwyn Morgan. That was a great match."

They headed out and joined the crowd walking across the bridge.

Franco Zefferelli's staging of *Much Ado About Nothing* was a big hit with London audiences. Sherry adored every minute of it, right through the curtain call. "I wish Lorena could have seen this.

"Perhaps she'll come back to London before the run is over." Jeremy kept a hand on her shoulder as they moved toward the exit.

"I loved how they put it together," Susan said. "Having the actors put their heads through the holes in the furniture so they could be the carvings was great."

"I don't always like it when they get clever with Shakespeare but Zefferelli pulled it off," Edward admitted. "Did you see his movie of Romeo and Juliet?"

Sherry nodded. Jeremy shook his head.

"It was fab," Susan said, her eyes dreamy. "They used a thirteen-year-old as Juliet."

Jeremy looked horrified. "That's ridiculous. No one knows what real love is at thirteen. I mean, at that age your hormones are out of control. Everything is too bright. Too hard felt." He tucked Sherry under his arm. "You have to be more mature to truly appreciate love."

Sherry shivered. What, she wondered, was he going to think when he found out how mature she was?

"I don't know about that," Susan said. "I'm eighteen and I think I know my own mind." She looked at Edward. "I know what I want when I see it. Anyway, everyone knows girls grow up faster than boys."

Sherry stifled a giggle.

Jeremy looked down at Sherry. They dropped back behind the others. "Do you know what you want?" he asked in a low intense voice.

She looked up at him. His eyes gleamed amber in the street light. "Yes. I know exactly what I want. But I don't think I can have it."

Jeremy enfolded her in his arms. He rested his chin on the top of her head. "If it is anything I have to give, it is yours."

"Oh god," Sherry muttered. She turned to face him. "Jeremy, we have to talk. There are some things you need to know about me."

"Come on you two," Edward called out. "The pub's going to close before we get a drink."

Jeremy studied Sherry's taut face. "Sherry's a bit tired. We're going straight home."

She took a deep breath. It was time to face the music. "I'll ring you about tomorrow, Susan." She pulled her iPhone out of her purse. "Give me your number."

"What is that?" Jeremy asked.

Sherry looked down and realized what she had done. She gasped and put it away. She scrabbled in her purse for a pencil and wrote Susan's number on the back of the playbill.

"See you tomorrow." Susan hugged her. She and Edward joined the crowd strolling toward the pub.

Jeremy reached over and took Sherry's purse. "That was a pretty thing." He pulled out the iPhone and turned it over in his hands.

Sherry tried to look at it from his perspective. A slim white cylinder. A black plastic screen on one side, surrounded by a white casing. The screen was dark. Even if she could have charged it, there wouldn't be any reception. She could have showed him the pictures though. And the games. She was sure Jeremy would like those, if he didn't run screaming.

"It's a new invention. It's not on the market yet. It won't be out for some time."

"How did you get it then?"

Sherry sighed. "It's a long story. Let's wait until were home. I think we might want to open a bottle of wine." She saw a flash of humor in Jeremy's eyes.

"I see no problem with that program." He hailed a taxi.

Sherry leaned back into the seat. When he got in, she snuggled up to him, putting her head on his shoulder. She captured his hands and held them tightly. This might be her last chance. By the end of tonight, he could kick her out, or perhaps, call Bedlam. She wondered if there was any chance that he might believe her. She lifted his hand to her cheek. Jeremy's fingers curled into hers.

Once they reached his flat, Sherry sat poker straight on the sofa while he poured them each a glass of wine. He lit the fire and turned on the stereo on low. The mellow strains of Mancini drifted through the room.

Jeremy sat beside her and shifted so they were face to face. He kissed away the frown between her eyebrows. "There is nothing you can tell me that will make any difference to the way I feel. I love you. I want you here with me. I will want you forever."

"Do you think you might still want me fifty years from now?" Sherry whispered.

Jeremy nodded gravely. "I think there is an extremely good chance I will want you one hundred years from now, medical science being what it is."

"It's not that good," Sherry said. "Not yet."

"Yes, well, I know that, but in the twenty-first century? One hundred years will be 2069. Lord, I wonder what we will be like?"

Sherry took a deep breath. "Well I don't know about 2069, but I can tell you about the first part of the twenty-first century."

Jeremy looked amused. "Oh, and why is that?"

"Because that's where I was last week. That's *when* I come from."

Jeremy snorted. "Right! Tell me another one."

"Jeremy, it's true." Sherry put down her wine glass. She clasped her hands together to keep them from shaking. "I know it sounds impossible but it's true."

Jeremy looked at her as if she'd grown a second head. "And why exactly did you decide to take a trip to the past? And *if*, you were going to take a trip to the past, why here? Why now? Why not somewhere really interesting?"

"I don't know why." Her smile trembled. "Maybe it was you."

Jeremy lifted an eyebrow and said nothing.

"That moment we kissed as strangers on the train was a moment of real magic." She looked at him, willing him to see the truth in her eyes. "You have no idea of how many times I wished I'd told you to call me."

She turned and stared at the fire. "But I was too much of a coward and I lost my chance. I went back to America and I lived out my life without you." She stared at her clasped hands. "Jeremy, I am sixty-three-years-old."

Jeremy raised an eyebrow. "I must say, you've aged well. You look about twenty. If your story were true, medicine made some miraculous advances."

He didn't believe her. She drew a shaky breath and continued. "Last week Lorena treated me to an adventure for my birthday. A Virtual Reality adventure."

"Come again?"

Sherry stumbled. This was harder than she thought. "Virtual reality is a game where you step into another world that seems as real as your own. Lorena said that this restaurant called The Castle had taken VR to a whole new level. We bought our tickets and we went to 1969 London."

Sherry willed her voice to stop shaking. "I thought it was a great simulation. The oddest part was we both looked young. I couldn't understand how a game could do that. And then we went to the pub and I saw you."

Jeremy looked as if he were thinking about soothing drinks.

"Look. I can prove it." She emptied her purse onto the coffee table. "Here is my driver's license. Look at my picture. Look at the date."

Jeremy ran his thumb over the license. "Born November fifth." He gave her a half smile. "Guy Fawkes Day. That's lucky . . . or not."

His thumb stilled. "Expires November fifth, 2017." For the first time he looked shaken. "This is a terrible picture of you," he said without looking up. "I mean, I know all drivers' license pictures are bad, but this one takes the biscuit. You look about fifty."

"It's not as bad as it looks." She took back the license. "After all, I was sixty when it was taken."

Jeremy stared at her face intently. He shook his head as if he were trying to clear it. "Impossible," he muttered.

Sherry reached into her purse and pulled her ticket out of its zippered compartment. "This is how I got here. It's my ticket home again."

He took it from her and ran his fingers over the ridged numbers. "Interesting." His voice revealed nothing. He reached for the iPhone and turned it over in his hand. "That's an iPhone." Sherry wished she could tell what he was thinking.

"And what's an iPhone when it's at home?"

"Oh boy," Sherry muttered. "How do I explain this?"

"Try."

"Okay." Sherry tried to sort her history in a logical sequence. "Back in the eighties or nineties, we put a lot of satellites in space."

"To be expected. So when did we colonize the moon?"

"We haven't."

Jeremy looked dumbfounded "How is that possible? The first moon landing was last July. Colonization is the next logical step."

"Yeah." Sherry sighed. "That didn't happen. We invented rockets that could land by themselves. Then in 1986 millions of people watched on TV as the Challenger blew apart after takeoff. It killed everyone aboard. It seemed that accident took the heart out of the space program."

"That's rather short sighted. I would think that colonizing other planets would be one of our important accomplishments." Jeremy leaned back, crossed his legs, and put his arms behind his head. "If we didn't colonize space, or blow ourselves up, what changed? Surely we did something wonderful?"

Sherry's head shot up. "You believe me?"

"Let's say I'm keeping an open mind on the subject. I have a tendency to believe six impossible things before breakfast." Jeremy smiled wryly. "I got into physics because of Einstein and H.G. Wells. I've also read Heinlein, Asimov, and E.E. Doc Smith."

"So have I." Sherry tried to catch a stray thought. Which book was it?

"When I was a kid, I was sure I was going to invent a time machine. You know it's a funny thing about science fiction." Jeremy stared into his wine glass. "I expect a lot of it to become true."

"Wait. Did you read all of Heinlein?"

"More than once." He gestured to the bookcase. "Half the bottom shelf is Heinlein. I've re-read almost all of them several times.

"Do you remember a book of his called *Space Cadet*? It's about these three friends at a space academy. I don't know when he wrote it. Forties or Fifties probably."

"Yeah, I read that."

"Do you remember when the hero gets to the academy? He opens his backpack and pulls out his personal communicator to call home?"

Jeremy nodded.

"That's what an iPhone is. A personal communicator. And do you remember the personal teaching devices?"

"A lot of authors wrote about those."

"Right. Those came into major use in the 1980s. They are called personal computers and they . . ."

Jeremy lifted his eyes to the ceiling. "Sherry, I know what a computer is. We had some very large ones at the lab where I used to work."

"Sorry. I forgot when they were invented." Sherry fumbled for dates in her mind. "Well, in the 1980s, I think, someone invented a microchip and it made computers a lot smaller and cheaper. They get cheaper all the time and they are all over the world. The computers can communicate with each other through satellite reception. They call it the Internet."

Jeremy said nothing.

"Most people don't write letters any more. They send mail on the Internet. It's called email. I could send an email from that phone." She couldn't stop rambling. If she gave him enough detail, surely he would believe her?

Jeremy picked up the phone again. "There is nothing here. How do you do it? Do you simply think at it?"

"It isn't charged. You can see the keyboard when it is charged."

The music stopped. The needle scratched softly as the turntable continued to revolve. Jeremy got up and lifted the needle. He stood with his back to her, looking at the bookcase. He swung round. "Please tell me there are still books. That is one science fiction thing I don't want to come true. I love the feel of paper. I don't want one of those reader things like they have in some sci-fi."

"Those readers exist. But so do paper books." She wanted to erase the frown line on his forehead. She summoned a smile. "I'm with you. I love holding a book too much to give up the paper kind."

"Well, that's a relief." He turned the record over and reset the needle. "What about food? Do you live on soy protein?"

"No. There's still food and wine and houses and cars and televisions and movies. None of that changed."

"I'm surprised."

Sherry giggled. "Well, it changed some. Special effects have come a long way and now everyone has DVD players and DVR so they can record their programs and not miss them."

Jeremy leaned back and looked at the fire. "Do we become more civilized? Or is terrorism still the favorite weapon of choice?"

"Ah well . . ." This was one question she didn't want to answer. Sherry was sure he was thinking about his brother and she didn't want to talk about 9/11 and its aftermath. "We've stopped trying to kill our politicians. Oh, except for Ronald Reagan, but that attempt didn't succeed."

"Ronald Reagan. The old movie actor? Why would anyone try to kill him?"

"Well, he was the President at the time."

Jeremy sighed. When he turned to her his eyes were bleak. "You should have stopped while you were ahead."

"What do you mean?"

"You expect me to believe a B movie actor became President of the United States? That's coming on a bit too strong."

"But it's true!"

Jeremy got up and switched off the music. He picked up the iPhone and her driver's license. "You said they have excellent special effects in California. I believe you. These are very good." He tossed them back to her.

Sherry's heart contracted. "I promise you. Everything I told you was true. Why would I lie to you?"

There was no warmth in his look. He seemed to have withdrawn behind an invisible screen. "You said you had a story I could use in my magazine. Was that what you wanted? To be in *Twenty-Eight*? Your fifteen minutes of fame?"

"Why would I want to be in your paper next to *Aliens from Mars*?" Sherry flashed back. "I neither want nor need fame. I wanted truth between us."

His stony expression told her everything she didn't want to know. It was over. She reached blindly for her cards and the iPhone and stuffed them back into her purse. "I love you," she whispered, "and I wanted you to know why I'll have to leave."

Jeremy's eyes softened. "Is that what this story's about?"

He reached for her hand. "Are you preparing me for our breakup? Don't do it yet."

He drew her up and into his arms. "Not yet. Come to bed." He led her unresisting up the stairs. They undressed without speaking and lay far apart.

Sherry stifled a sob. Jeremy rolled across the bed and pulled her into his arms. He kissed the tears from her face. "I don't understand why you would tell me those ridiculous faradiddles, but it doesn't change what I feel for you. I will love you to the day I die." He paused. "I don't suppose you know the exact date do you?"

Sherry resented the note of humor in his voice. "Jeremy! I am not a fortuneteller or a mind reader. What I told you was the absolute truth."

"Of course it was. How would you like to have lunch with me at the office tomorrow? See where all that news comes from?"

Sherry knew he was brushing her off, trying to change the subject. She seethed silently. "What if I do give you a story?"

"You already did." Jeremy snickered. "'Future girl says B movie actor to become President.'" That headline is an example of the best of *Twenty-Eight*."

"Not that story. Another one."

"I like your stories." Jeremy spooned her into him. "They are very amusing. You should write science fiction."

Sherry cradled her head into his chest. "I am not making it up," she whispered, "and some way I am going to prove it to you."

Jeremy yawned. "Tomorrow," he mumbled. "Lunch. Love you . . ." His voice trailed off into sleep.

Sherry lay wide-awake trying to think of one significant thing that would happen in the near future. One thing that would absolutely prove the truth of her story. Nothing came to mind. She had years of future history in her head. It was all a jumble. When had George Wallace been shot? She'd forgotten about him. How about Apartheid in South Africa? She sighed. She was pretty sure that remained in effect until the nineties. Princess Di? No. That was about fifteen years in the future. There had to be something. As she drifted off into sleep, her last waking thought was the ticket. Could he go forward?

Chapter 22
Lorena

"Where do you live?" Lorena asked.

"On Manhattan, between Fifth and Sixth Street."

"Oh," Lorena said. She was busy staring at the 1969 version of Fairfax Avenue.

Fairfax High School and Canter's Deli were the same. Many of the buildings had changed. The Farmer's Market at the corner of Third and Fairfax looked different. So did Du-Pars.

She tore her gaze away from the buildings and looked at Dave. She re-memorized his profile. She leaned over and put a tentative hand on his thigh. He covered it with his own. She sighed happily and leaned back.

Third Street was a parade of beautiful homes. Lorena turned to look back at a mansion with a tennis court surrounded by a crayon yellow adobe wall. "Odd choice of color."

"What?"

"That house back there. With the wall that looks like a giant lemon."

"Bizarre, isn't it? I love to walk by that one and try to figure out what kind of people live there. I want to use it in a story."

"You walk?" Lorena craned her neck looking for pedestrians. No people to be seen. "You must be the only one."

"Yeah. Walking's a sport that hasn't caught on in Los Angeles. I got stopped by the police once. They wanted to know where my car was."

Lorena snorted.

Manhattan Street was a step down. No. Scratch that. A whole staircase down from the elegant homes on Third Street.

Dave parked in front of a dowdy brick building. "Home sweet home." He led her down the hall to a faded orange door and unlocked it.

She stepped into a living room that had seen better days. Probably around the turn of the century.

The living room led into a narrow kitchen furnished with a green Formica topped table and two ripped plastic chairs.

An uninspired still life of orange flowers graced the dingy cream wall above the worn mustard colored sofa. The scratched plastic coffee table held a radio and a small black and white television. Brown fake wood side tables with gold speckled, white china lamps and a profusion of books completed the décor. No wonder he'd never talked about it.

She walked over to the only other door and peered inside.

A bathroom floored with cracked white diamond shaped tiles. The chipped bathtub had a mildew stained white curtain around it. A built in mirror and a plastic toothbrush holder hung above the discolored sink. She turned back to the living room. "Nice," she commented. "Did you do your own decorating?"

Dave laughed. "I rented it furnished. I was lucky to get it. It's seventy dollars a month, which fits my budget."

Lorena swiveled as she surveyed the room. Something was missing. "Where's the bed?"

"Don't you think that might be a tad premature," Dave asked her gravely.

Lorena blushed. "You know what I mean. Where do you sleep? That couch doesn't look very comfortable."

"Ah, the wonders of the modern world," Dave said. He walked over to one of the closet doors opposite the sofa and opened it. There were bedsprings sticking out. "Behold." He pulled them down and a bed popped into view.

"A Murphy bed! I didn't think those existed anymore."

"Well they do. I myself was somewhat surprised. But I have grown very attached to it. I like the eccentric."

Was he referring to her? Lorena moved away from the bed. Her nerves hummed. She sat on the sofa and clasped her hands together so he wouldn't see them shaking. "It's a very nice bed."

"Yes," Dave said, looking her over, "very nice indeed. So what's next? Are you going to tell me the truth?"

Zero hour. Lorena looked away. If she only knew how to begin? "Have you read much time travel fiction?"

"I've read some, Heinlein's *Door into Summer*, H.G. Well's *The Time Machine*." Dave sat next to her. "My new favorite is Harry Harrison's *The Technicolor Time Machine*."

"I haven't read that," Lorena admitted.

Dave sorted through the books on the table. "Here." He offered her a paperback. "I picked it up a couple of weeks ago at a second hand bookstore."

"Thanks." The cover picture was a bright blue splash with curlicues of black and white striped ribbon. "So do you think time travel is possible?"

Leaning back, Dave crossed his arms behind his head, and stared at the ceiling. "Einstein said something about time and space being figments of our imagination, but I can't wrap my mind around it."

"Try," she whispered.

His eyes sharpened. "Why?"

Lorena's hands clenched on the book. "In July 1972, I will meet a man named David Cramer. One month from our first meeting we will be married. And," she looked up with a twisted smile, "we will live happily ever after until . . ." Her voice broke.

"Until?"

"You died."

Dave stared at her. "You want me to believe you time traveled?"

Lifting her chin, Lorena returned his look. "It's the truth".

He reached for her hand and massaged her tense fingers. "How? Why?"

She curled her fingers around his. "One day last week, I treated my best friend Sherry to this place called The Castle, which was supposed to have this great virtual reality game . . ."

"Come again?" Dave interrupted. "What's that?"

Lorena was stumped for a moment. How do you explain something that hasn't been thought of yet? "It's a kind of made up world which seems totally real while you are in it. You can walk around and do and see things that aren't real."

"I get it," Dave said. "Kind of Disneyland on LSD?"

Lorena giggled as the image of a drug crazed Mickey took shape in her mind. "That is so wrong, but yes, kind of like that. Sherry wanted the world to be London in 1969, so we bought our tickets and we went in and it was . . . amazing. It felt so real. Then Sherry met a man she had actually known in 1969. That's when we knew it wasn't virtual reality at all. It was time travel."

Dave's hand tightened over hers. She waited for him to say something. He remained silent, his expression unreadable.

"Sherry wanted to stay," Lorena continued. "I didn't. So I went back to the future." She tried to stifle a nervous giggle. "In the 1980's a movie is going to come out called *Back to the Future*. You are going to love it. We both will."

She looked at Dave's face. It was a mask. Lorena wished he'd say something. Anything. What was she going to do if he didn't believe her? "When I got home, I remembered something. Something you said when you were dying. About a scrapbook and our wedding picture." A familiar coldness crept over her. "I'd forgotten what you said. After you died, I didn't think about anything. It was enough just to get through the day."

Dave put a comforting arm around her.

Lorena turned in his embrace. "I know this is hard. If I weren't here, if I hadn't gone through the door, I wouldn't believe it either. But . . ." She reached into her purse and pulled out the carefully folded letter. "You wrote this and left it for me.

He glanced at the note and froze. "This is my handwriting or a damn good imitation."

"It's yours. Read it."

He read it twice. He looked up and smiled faintly. "What a jerk! I didn't finish the letter."

"I think that was your sense of humor working. It's part of your charm." If he didn't say something she was going to scream. "Well?"

"Well, it seems clear enough." He motioned toward the Murphy bed. "Shall we?"

She pushed him away. "*Now* you're being a jerk! You don't know me yet."

"But I will." He leaned over to kiss her. Her lips met his eagerly. The kiss grew hotter.

What am I doing? Lorena broke the kiss. "David, I know you will love me. But I don't think you love me right now and I am not going to give my virginity to a man who does not love me."

Dave's eyes were still dark with passion but her words acted like ice water. "You're a virgin? How is that possible? I thought we got married."

"We did, but not in 1969, and I am damn sure you were my first."

Dave looked skeptical.

Lorena raised her eyebrows. "You don't think this is how I look in the future, do you? Whatever sent me through time made me young again and I am fairly sure that means virgin."

Dave flopped down on the sofa. "Wow! This requires some thought."

Lorena sat down next to him.

He reached over and twirled a lock of her hair around his finger. A gesture so familiar it brought tears to her eyes. "Okay," he said, "how are we going to handle this?"

Her body reacted to the heat in his eyes. "I don't know." Her hand stole into his. "Maybe we could get to know each other a little better first." She leaned her head against his shoulder. "You know what's funny? For the rest of our lives together, you are going to know all about these two weeks. And I am not going to remember a thing. What is happening now is a part of your future and a part of my present."

Dave came to attention. "Two weeks? Why two weeks? Why don't we stay together till the meeting you remember?"

"David, look at your note. It says two weeks. So that's how long we have."

He picked up the note and read it again. He dropped it back on the table. "We could drive to Vegas," he offered, "and get married now?"

Lorena thought about it for a minute. "No." She shook her head. "We didn't do that. I have no memory of it."

He sighed and looked at the bed.

She shook her head.

"Get to know each other, huh?"

Lorena nodded.

"Okay, wife to be," he pulled her to her feet, "let's catch a movie at Grauman's Chinese. Afterward, I'll take you to CC Brown's for a hot fudge sundae. Is that an acceptable first date?"

She nodded wordlessly and flung her arms around him.

He reached down and claimed her lips. The kiss started out friendly. Lorena clasped her hands behind his head and drew him closer. Time stopped.

This time it was Dave who broke away. "I still have some vestige of sanity," he said hoarsely. "If we keep this up, we are never going to make it past this bed. Come on let's go."

Chapter 23
Sherry

Considering how Jeremy dressed for work, Sherry assumed *Twenty-Eight's* office would be impressive. Not the hodgepodge of battered desks placed back to back she saw before her.

She edged in, avoiding the phone wires tangled in the aisles, waiting to trip the unwary. Most of the desks were occupied by people banging away on upright typewriters. A few of them had phones tucked between their ear and shoulder. The clatter of the keys competed with the chitter of the ticker tape spitting out a continual stream of narrow white paper. A buzz of conversation filled the room.

A pimpled young man who looked as if he should still be in high school wove his way through the office with a tea tray. Reporters snagged cups without looking up.

Jeremy beckoned him over. The boy's face flushed bright red at the sight of Jeremy. He stumbled and caught himself. "It's—it's not very hot sir. I could make a fresh pot."

"Sherry, this is Giles Weatherby, our office general all around man. He is working his way up to reporter." Jeremy drew Sherry forward. "Giles, this is Sherry, my girl from the Future."

Sherry gave him a kick. "Stop it."

The wave of color flushed Giles's blond scalp. "Pleased to meet you." He held out his hand.

Sherry shook it, ignoring its dampness. She remembered the agonies of self-consciousness that went with being seventeen and smiled at him encouragingly. "So you're going to be a writer."

Giles stuck out his chin. "I already am a writer. I want to be a writer who is paid to do it."

"Does Jeremy treat you well or is he a secret slave driver?"

"Oh no! He's super," Giles assured her. "This is a great place to work."

"Jeremy!" The weather-beaten man at the far desk waved his hand. "Over here." The man typed one fingered and ate a bun at the same time. Crumbs sprinkled his shirt. He looked as if he hadn't shaved in a week.

"I've got another sighting of the Ghost Abbot in Prestbury. Also a ghost of a Cavalier riding horseback. Mrs. . . ." He consulted his notes. "Mrs. Puddleman heard the clopping of horse's hooves and looked out her window. Gave her quite a turn."

A brassy haired, pug-faced woman with a phone tucked under her chin interrupted. "Forget that, Peter. Some fisherman out of Liverpool says he captured a live mermaid."

"We'll run them both," Jeremy said. "Laurel, get a mermaid picture out of stock. Peter, get up to Prestbury."

Peter stood up and dusted the crumbs off his shirt. "I love that place, they have more sightings than anywhere else in England."

"I've got a story myself," Jeremy said. "This is Sherry. She comes from the future."

"Shut. Up." Sherry emphasized her words with a discreet kick on his ankle.

Peter's shaggy eyebrows lifted. The pug-faced woman looked up and eyed Sherry as if she were a fresh tea biscuit.

Sherry turned to Jeremy. "I don't want you to print anything I said. Not anything." She pulled his head down to her level and glared at him. "Are you listening, Smythe?

I didn't tell you any of that so you could put it in your magazine."

"Right," Jeremy said, grabbing her hand, "come see my office."

He led her to a battered glass door with the word Editor stenciled in gold and ushered her inside.

The institutional white walls featured framed covers of *Twenty-Eight*. Almost invisible among the garish magazine covers was a small photo of a castle with tall square towers set in a field of Technicolor green. In the corner of the office an aspidistra drooped disconsolately.

"Plant killer, are you?"

Jeremy nodded. He seated himself behind the mahogany desk and glanced at his messages. "My mum keeps sending me plants. She says I need more green in my life. Don't know why."

Sherry sat on the brown leather sofa and tried to relax. "As a matter of fact, research has discovered that plants in an indoor environment are very good for humans. They clear the air and are calming to the senses."

Jeremy looked at the aspidistra, revolted. "I defy anyone to be calm with that in the room." He looked at Sherry straight faced. "Although, with a little help, it makes a wonderful alien."

"Is that what you did with the dead ones? Turn them into aliens?"

"One of them. The others were interred in the rubbish."

Sherry studied the aspidistra. "Okay, I'll give you creepy. You need a better class of plant." Two silver framed pictures on the desk caught her eye. She crossed behind Jeremy to study them. The first was a photo of a cricket team. Jeremy knelt in the first row. She ran a loving finger over his smile She moved on to the next picture. A family shot. Jeremy stood between Jen and a young man with blond hair and a beautiful serious smile. Rob, of course. The brother who died. Her mother's heart ached for the parents. "Jen's hair is shorter here so I'm guessing this is a couple of years ago." She pointed to the dark haired sprite holding a cocker spaniel in her arms. Her hair was razor cut into streaks and her eyes promised mischief. "What's your other sister's name?"

"That's Courtney. She hasn't decided whether she is going to be the next prime minister or a vet. That's Mum, of course, and Dad."

Sherry imagined that was how Jeremy would look in forty years. Silver haired and gorgeous. "What does he do now that he turned the magazine over to you? He looks far too young to retire."

"Oh well, he dabbles in politics a bit." Jeremy's voice trailed off. "Come on, Sherry, sit down." He dragged a comfortable looking easy chair in front of the desk and pushed her into it, kissing the top of her head. He put a sheet of carbon paper between two pieces of typing paper and rolled them into the typewriter.

"Wow! I had forgotten all about that. Do you know how long it has been since I have seen carbon paper?"

Jeremy looked at her searchingly. "You are good," he muttered. "Okay," he said, fingers poised, "tell me how it feels to be pulled back in time."

Sherry could feel the hot burn of temper making its way to her face. "This discussion is over." She stood and stormed out of his office, slamming the door behind her.

"Sherry, come back!"

She heard his phone ring and his voice barking, "Smythe here. Make it quick." She kept walking through the noise and clatter of the outer office. She could barely see the way to the elevators through her tears.

Jeremy caught up with her as she stepped onto the street. He pulled her back as a passing mini almost grazed her.

"What are you doing?" he shouted. "Trying to get yourself killed? This is London! You have to watch where you're going."

She shuddered at the near miss. "I wasn't paying attention," she said with a sniffle. "I was trying to decide what to do."

He turned her around and gathered her into his arms. "You need to be more careful," he said, burying his face into her hair. "I aged ten years before I grabbed you."

Sherry's nerves zinged. She laid her head on his chest. The rapid beating of his heart thrummed in her ears.

There were both oblivious of the stares they were attracting.

A whistle broke through their consciousness. "I'd like some of that."

They broke apart. Jeremy caught the eyes of the whistler. "This one's mine. Get your own." He looked down at Sherry with a half-smile. "Lunch?"

She nodded.

Jeremy took her to the journalist club. It was very brown and elegant. People spoke in hushed whispers. The tablecloths were white. The china, bone thin. The waiters obsequious.

The headwaiter knew Jeremy and greeted him warmly, leading them to a table at the window.

Sherry looked around. "I'm surprised they let you in here considering what you publish."

Jeremy laughed. "It's hereditary. I got my father's table when he retired. I used to come here with him on school holiday. At the time I knew I would be a great scientist. I never thought about taking over the magazine."

Sherry pretended to study the ornate menu, not really interested in food. "What did you used to order?"

"Roast beef and Yorkshire pudding with Trifle to follow."

Sherry was too upset to eat, but she forced a smile. "Sounds good. I'll have that."

He ordered for them both and turned back to her.

She played with the ornate crystal water glass, her head bent.

He leaned over and lifted her chin. "I am truly sorry," he said softly. "It was inexcusable to goad you like that. But that story you told me . . ."

Sherry hated the frustrated look in his eyes. "Jeremy, I know how it sounds, but . . ."

His lips tightened. "It feels as though you are lying to me and I cannot bear lies."

She nodded dejectedly. "I don't blame you. If it hadn't happened to me, I don't think I'd believe me either. It's too bizarre. But please try to believe this much. I love you with all my heart and I would never lie to you."

Jeremy caught her hand and began absently stroking it. "Okay. Maybe it wasn't a lie. Let's call it fiction?"

Sherry's eyes sparked. "It's the truth, dammit."

He said nothing. She could see the concern in his eyes.

The lump in her throat made it had to form words. "Jeremy, I can't stay here with you. I have to go back to . . . to where I came from."

Jeremy's fingers tightened around hers. "Why?"

"Because there are things that happened in my future I cannot have taken away."

Jeremy looked at her searchingly and waited for her to continue.

Sherry took a deep breath. "In 1976, I got married." Jeremy's grip turned to iron. She tried to pull her hand away. "Jeremy, don't. You're hurting me."

His grasp softened.

The waiter brought the food. Sherry smiled up at the waiter. "It all looks lovely."

Jeremy waited for him to leave. His eyes looked hard. "So in this future of yours, you got married. Was he the great love you were waiting for?"

"No!" She reached across the table and touched his lips with her fingertips. "Jeremy, you are my great love. You're everything I ever dreamed of."

He caught her fingers and kissed them. "Stay," he whispered. "We can forget all of this."

"I can't stay! I have two children." She swallowed the tears clogging her throat. "If I stay, John and Michael would cease to exist. I cannot make them unborn."

"And your husband? Do you miss him?"

"I don't care about Bill. We've been divorced for twenty-three years. "I would stay with you now and forever except for John and Michael." Sherry leaned forward, her hands white knuckled. "John is married now. They're expecting a child in June. How could I possibly wink my sons and my unborn grandchild out of existence?"

"And what about us?"

Sherry would have given anything to erase the pain she heard in his voice. She raised her eyes, pleading for understanding. "What if it had been your mother and father? What if one of them went back in time and met someone else? You wouldn't have been born, Jeremy. I could not bear that. I will not do that to my children."

Jeremy turned to stone. "When are you leaving?"

"Soon."

"How long?"

"A few days." Sherry reached across the table and caught his hand. Her purse fell to the floor. She released his hand and bent over and picked it up. The tickets. What if Jeremy could see for himself?

She looked up. "Jeremy, I want you to come with me to the door where I entered this time."

"And watch you go?"

"No. I want you to try and come ahead with me."

Jeremy stared at her.

"Just for a little while," she pleaded. "A brief visit. I want you to know what I am telling you is true."

"How brief?"

"A day. Maybe two."

Jeremy considered it through pursed lips. He nodded. "I could do that. I could free up for a few days but not until after the cricket match."

"You're putting me off for a cricket match?" He still didn't believe her.

"I'm bloody well not going to tell them I'm sidelined because I have to pay a visit to the future," Jeremy growled.

"But you'll come after that? I don't know if it will work," Sherry babbled, "but it ought to. I have an extra ticket."

"I will follow you." The beginnings of a smile lurked in his eyes. "I suppose if you asked me to, I would follow you to hell."

Sherry gasped in relief. "It isn't hell, I promise you, and I know you can get back here."

"But you will be staying."

Sherry felt a bubble of panic rise up. "No! I'll be coming back here with you. I can't leave you yet. I need more time."

"Is everything satisfactory?" The waiter gazed at their untouched plates.

Jeremy looked at Sherry. "I think we are not quite as hungry as we thought. Could you pack this up and bring us a pot of tea?"

Sherry tried to smile. "In England tea solves everything doesn't it?"

"Not everything, but it helps." Jeremy's eyes never left her face. "Come back to the office with me. I don't want to let you out of my sight."

Sherry nodded. She wanted to spend every waking minute with him. There were so few of them left.

Chapter 24
Lorena

Lorena tickled Dave's nose with a feather that had escaped from the pillow. His nose twitched. He reached out for her and cradled her in to his body. Lorena gloried in the feel of him.

Her vow of celibacy hadn't lasted past the first night. Her body had been new to loving, but her mind remembered. David had always been everything she ever wanted in a lover.

The delight was that she seemed to be everything he'd ever wanted. His feelings were in his eyes and the way he touched her.

"Wake up, sleepyhead." She fluttered kisses on his eyes.

"No. I'm having a great dream. His eyes stayed closed as he lifted her on top of him. "This girl came into my life and said she was my future. Then we had the best sex I ever had in my life."

"Oh. Well, I don't want to wake you. It would be cruel." She captured his lips. Lorena could feel parts of him were definitely awake.

Dave's arms pulled her closer "That's all right," he murmured. "Come on in. We'll share the dream."

Afterward they shared the shower.

"So what do you want to do today?" David lounged against the bathroom door watching her try to pull a comb through her long hair.

"Ouch!" Lorena gave up the struggle and glared at him. "I want to go to the drugstore. I can't believe you don't have any conditioner."

"Hey, real guys don't use that kind of stuff." He walked in the living room and found his pack of Winstons. "We could drive to the beach. I've got a full tank of gas and we can get corn dogs."

"Corn dogs? Bleagh." She took away the cigarettes and kissed him. "You know what I want to do tonight? I want to eat at the Hat."

"The Brown Derby? I'm sorry, kiddo. Grad assistant salary doesn't run to that kind of meal."

"Well, successful writer royalties do," Lorena replied smugly, "and I brought money with me."

"You're a writer?"

"No, my darling, I'm the actor. You're the writer."

Dave sat down. He looked stunned. "You mean I get published. I mean I thought . . . I hoped . . ."

"And you do. You have the awards to prove it."

Dave looked like Santa had landed on the roof. "I get awards?" He patted the seat beside him. "Come here. Sit down and tell me all about me."

Lorena sat and cuddled in to him. "No. It's not good for you to know too much about your future."

Dave started tickling her.

"No, stop. Stop!" She wriggled away. "Tell you what. I'll tell you two things tonight at dinner. We'll make it a celebration."

Lorena took in the giant brown cement hat fronted with a brick colored awning. "I love it." She craned her neck to look up at the Derby shaped sign *'Eat at The Hat'*. "The sign looks like it's sitting on a water tower. I wonder why?"

"It may have had something to do with the dome air conditioning. The Brown Derby was one of the first air conditioned buildings in Los Angeles back in the thirties."

Lorena was intrigued. "How do you know that?"

Dave shrugged. "Read it somewhere. I like odd facts. They also used to keep live chickens on the premises. They used to have a slogan on the menu 'Chicken whose feet never touched the ground.'"

Lorena shuddered. "That's gross. I'm not ordering anything with chicken." She slipped her arm through Dave's. "Come on. I'm starved."

The Maître d' showed them to a circular padded leather booth and handed them menus.

"Hey, this isn't too bad," Dave said. "I thought it would be more expensive. Meatloaf. $3.50. I like meatloaf."

"Look, it's George Burns." Lorena pointed at one of the many framed caricatures above their booth. "And there's Bob Hope." She scanned the other booth looking at the pictures. "I don't recognize half these people."

Dave grinned. "Last year Andy Warhol said everybody was going to get their fifteen minutes of fame. Maybe he ate here once and that's where he got the idea."

A tuxedoed waiter brought them a cloth covered breadbasket and took their drink orders.

Dave lifted the napkin covering the bread. Heat wafted up from the thin dark buttery cheese sprinkled slices. He sampled one. "This is great." He leaned over and offered Lorena a bite.

She closed her eyes to better appreciate the flavor. "Mmmm. Heaven. I could make a meal off this. But I have to have a Cobb Salad. It was invented here."

"I thought you weren't going to order anything with chicken."

"It's leftover chicken," she said defensively. "If I don't eat it, they'll throw the poor thing out. Besides," she added, looking around the circular room full of linen draped tables and red padded chairs, "I don't see any cages. Maybe they quit doing that."

The waiter brought their drinks and took their food order.

Dave lit a cigarette and glanced at the lantern-shaded chandeliers. "I could get used to this."

Lorena tried not to look like a tourist while scoping out the other diners. "Look! There's Carol Burnett. She's my hero."

Dave peered in the direction Lorena was looking. A waiter was carrying a telephone to a booth.

She jabbed him. "Not like that," she whispered "You have to look like you're not looking."

Dave grinned at her. "I actually understood that." He offered the breadbasket to Lorena. "Pay attention to me. You promised you'd tell me about my writing."

Lorena tore her attention away from their fellow diners. She took a piece of the offered bread. "Well, the first one was the Hugo." She bit into the cheesy goodness. "This bread is amazing," she mumbled. "I wonder if I could get the recipe."

Dave's eyes lit up. "I get a Hugo? What for?"

"It was for a novella. *The Wayfarer.* It's about . . ."

Dave looked like he'd been hit with a brick. "I know what it's about. I wrote *The Wayfarer* for my short story class my senior year. Professor Davidson said it showed promise, but the way he said it . . . I don't know if I even kept a copy."

"You did. It's in your mother's attic in a box marked *books.* You'll find it and you'll rewrite it." Lorena sipped her wine, enjoying Dave's look of bemusement. "But your biggest hit was a book you wrote for Claire called *Missing.* It was so popular that Doubleday gave you a five-book contract for a series. The hero was a sixteen-year-old girl who was trying to find her family after they were lost during a virtual reality vacation on Mars and . . ." Lorena stopped, thunderstruck. "Virtual Reality. Damn! You knew!"

"I did?" Dave asked cautiously. He looked at her as if she were a bomb that might explode, if not handled carefully. "What did I know?"

"You used what I told you about The Castle and created

a story out of it." She rested her chin in her hands. "This is so circular. You used what I told you about my future in our past. I can't wrap my head around it."

"Don't try," Dave advised her. "My brain is crossing just thinking about it."

The waiter brought their food. They stopped talking about the future and enjoyed the meal and each other.

"I don't know how you can say Charles Dickens is a better writer than Shakespeare," Lorena argued.

"Shakespeare was a hack. He stole most of his plots." Dave polished off the last bite of grapefruit cake.

The glint in Dave's eyes told Lorena he loved making her bristle. "Look who's talking," she retorted. "Remember where you got *Missing*. Who do you think you are?"

Dave's eyes twinkled "Rhetoric," he quoted. "Game and match!"

Lorena giggled. "I love *Rosencrantz & Guildenstern Are Dead*. I saw it in New York three times. I had a friend at the box office."

Dave agreed. "It was here at the Music Center in April. I got student tickets and went twice." He reached for his pack of Winstons.

Lorena firmed her lips, but the words came out anyway. "I wish you didn't smoke."

He tapped out a cigarette. "Why? I like it and everyone does it."

"Yeah, well everyone doesn't get cancer." She bit her lip. She hadn't meant to say that.

He froze. Put the pack down slowly as if it were a snake poised to bite him. "Is that what happened? I died of lung cancer?

Lorena nodded. Two tears squeezed out and trailed wetly down her cheeks.

Dave brushed them away with a gentle finger. "I gather no one's discovered a cure for cancer."

"Some cancers are curable, some are not." Lorena drew a ragged breath, willing the blackness away. "You hung on an extra year because of the state of the art of medicine. But there was a lot of pain for both of us."

"That seems so . . . It's hard to imagine your own death." He picked up the cigarette and lit it. "I was old though. That's a good thing."

Lorena slapped the cigarette out of his hand. "Not. Old. Enough!" Her eyes flamed. "Listen you jerk, do you know what it is like to have to watch someone struggle for every breath? To know you can't breathe for them? To watch your heart slip away?" Her voice broke. "You were god damned not old enough! I wanted another thirty years with you."

The waiter brought the check. Lorena reached into her purse and counted out the money in seething silence.

Dave took a deep breath. "I don't think humans are made to imagine our own deaths. Or even remember them. Empirically, I hear what you're saying, but I don't believe it."

Lorena started to protest.

Dave leaned over and hushed her with a kiss. "I don't believe you, but I will quit. I haven't been smoking very long. I only took it up in grad school." He took his pack of cigarettes and placed them on the table. "Maybe the waiter will take them as part of his tip."

Lorena looked at Dave with wonder. Joy welled up inside her.

"What are you thinking?" Dave asked.

"Did you ever have a moment so perfect you wanted to capture it in crystal?"

"Yeah." Dave looked across at Lorena. "Did you ever have a moment when the center of your universe changed?" He reached for her hand. "Let's change time. Stay."

Chapter 25
Sherry

The cricket match was as bewildering to Sherry as she thought it would be. She smiled and cheered when Susan did, but the trip to the future looped a pattern in her mind leaving very little space for cricket.

They broke for lunch at the end of the first half of the inning.

Jeremy handed her a ham sandwich and a bottle of Orange Squash. "Enjoying yourself?"

"Sure," she lied. "I like watching you have fun. It's kind of like watching another species."

"They are good," he said, referring to the opposing team, "but I think Edward will bowl them out properly if he can manage to take his eyes off Susan."

"She doesn't look too young for him now," Sherry whispered. Susan's new coat and hat made her look like a young Glynis Johns. "I bet he proposes tonight."

"I think he should wait. She's too young. You, on the other hand, are exactly the right age." He waggled his eyebrows and twirled an imaginary mustache. "Why don't we postpone this trip of yours and I'll show you my very best proposal."

Sherry forced a smile. "Wait till you see how old I really am. You'll run screaming."

The sun was setting by the time the match was over.

Jeremy helped her into the Aston Martin and got in. He yawned. "Well, where to? Show me this place."

"No. Not yet. Let's go home first. You can have a shower and change. There's no real hurry."

"Scared?" he asked, not unkindly.

"Terrified," Sherry admitted. "I am not sure it will work. I'm not sure it's a good idea for you to go to the future. Maybe we shouldn't do this."

"I don't think we are going to do anything." Jeremy started the car. "But I love you and therefore I am willing to see."

Jeremy stepped out of the shower. He poked his head in the bedroom while toweling his hair. "Anything special I should wear to the future? I don't have any Buck Rogers clothes."

Panic and naked need swirled through Sherry. What if this was the last time?

She grabbed him and pushed him onto the bed. Burying her face in his chest, she lost herself in the warmth and scent of him. She lingered on his nipple licking, pulling and tugging with her teeth. She could feel his passion rise to meet hers.

He slipped her sweater up and tugged it off. His lips teased hers until the kiss deepened into aching desire. Pleasure ripped through her. The storm whirled between them, consuming them both. They spiraled into completion together.

Jeremy collapsed on top of her, resting his forehead on hers. "Will I ever get enough of you?"

His breath tickled her cheek. She reached up and gently curled a strand of his hair around her fingers.

He rose up, supporting himself on his elbows. "Sherry, forget this nonsense. Stay here and marry me."

Every fiber of her being wanted to say yes. Guilt stabbed her. She was hurting him and she never meant to do that. "If there was a way I could stay without making my sons unborn I would do it in a heartbeat." She reached up and stroked his face. "I think we had better try to go. I need to let you see what I told you is true."

Jeremy's face shuttered. He sighed and rolled to his feet. "I'll get dressed."

She followed him to his closet. She picked out a white dress shirt and a pair of jeans for him and added a brown leather jacket. "Wear these. You won't stand out."

Jeremy took the offered clothes. "This is a sad commentary on the state of future fashion. I thought we would be wearing some kind of new fabric by the twenty-first century, maybe silver sheet metal, beaten soft."

"Nope," Sherry said from the bathroom. "Jeans are still worn."

She emerged from the bathroom, neat and tidy, her face composed. "Shall we go?"

Saturday night traffic jammed Argyle Street. Jeremy found a parking place two blocks away. He helped Sherry out of the car, retaining possession of her hand in a strong grip. "Lead on, MacDuff."

They walked, hands swinging, until they came to the shabby green door. Jeremy surveyed it with a frown. "This is your time machine? It's only a door."

Sherry went up the steps and pointed at the tiny signs.

He stooped down and read out loud, "The Castle. Please use ticket."

Sherry fished in her purse and brought out the ticket. As she slid it in, the slot gave off a green glow. There was a click. The door swung open. The slot in the second door glowed bright.

"I don't believe it," Jeremy said under his breath. His eyes wore their 'reporter' look. He followed her into the tiny hall, shutting the door behind him leaving them in darkness.

Sherry fed the two tickets to the second door. The sweep of blue light played over them.

Jeremy gave a little grunt of pain.

"What's wrong?" she asked, wishing she could see his face.

"Just a little twinge. I feel a bit weird."

Sherry's heart pounded. "Are you sure you want to do this? We can go back."

"No turning back." Jeremy's voice sounded strong. "I want to see what happens next."

The door swung wide to reveal a dimly lit hall."

"Not very imaginative, is it?" Jeremy reached for Sherry's hand and gripped it tightly. "I expected something more in line with Dr. Who's Police Box."

'Wait." She led him through the hall to the brightly lit computer room. They stopped dead, looking at each other with stunned amazement.

"You look old," they said in unison.

"Well, I am old," Sherry said. "I told you that. But you shouldn't be. Oh God, what have I done?"

She dragged him to a mirror. Side by side they were a beautiful couple. A beautiful couple in their sixties.

Jeremy's hair was more silver than ginger. Weather-beaten lines marked his face. Those amazing blue eyes were cradled in wrinkles. Jeremy seemed to have lost the ability to speak. He traced her face with his finger, lingering on each line. He looked into her eyes and ran a wondering hand over her head moving on to her shoulder, down her arm. His hand finally reached hers.

She waited for him to say something. Anything.

"Well, that settles it." His smile crinkled the corners of his eyes. "There will never be a day when you do not steal my breath away. You look wonderful."

Sherry gave a gasp of relief and wrapped her arms

around him. "I am sorry, Jeremy. I didn't think about time working both ways. I didn't think you would change."

He dropped a fleeting kiss on top of her head and studied himself in the mirror. "It's strange. I don't feel all that different. I would have thought that by sixty, I'd be bent and cracked with age."

"You look like your father and he's a fox."

Jeremy winced. "Please don't put that image in my head. One's father should never be a fox." He rolled his shoulders experimentally and winced. "Aside from some minor pain, I still feel like me at twenty-five."

Sherry's smile wavered. "Welcome to your sixties. That's the thing about getting old. Only your outer shell changes."

He gave a half laugh. "Come on, future girl, let's get out of here. I want to see where you live. I want to see what this future looks like."

Sherry led him down the passage to the front hall. "I'm going to have to call a cab unless Lorena can pick us up." She pulled out her iPhone and pressed a button. "Damn, I forgot it was dead. I'll charge it when I get home."

Jeremy regarded the phone skeptically. "Yes, do," he murmured, "I am looking forward to that."

She asked the doorman to call them a cab.

Jeremy gazed into the dining rooms. "Things don't look any different than 1969."

"Yes." Sherry had a hard time taking her eyes off Jeremy. He was still so beautiful. Why couldn't women age like men? "Well, we still build buildings the same way. I suppose some of the new skyscrapers are different, but in general I think we build the same. Maybe a little stronger. Every time we have an earthquake, engineers learn something new."

"Earthquakes. Hmmm. You know that is one of those phenomena I've never wished to experience." He gave an uneasy glance around. "Are you expecting one any time soon."

She shrugged. "Earthquakes are one of Nature's little surprises. We haven't learned to predict them."

They stepped outside. A hot wind rustled the palm trees. She could feel her skin drying in response.

"Is Los Angeles always this hot in November? It is still November, isn't it?"

Sherry stifled a giggle. They'd traveled into the future and he was talking about the weather? "Yes, it's November and no, it's not usually this hot. The Santa Ana winds are blowing."

Jeremy took off his jacket. "I feel like Lawrence of Arabia. I need one of those thingy's Peter O'Toole wore in the movie."

Heat roiled downward as she pictured him in those white robes. *Oh yes!*

Jeremy caught her expression. "You're thinking of another game aren't you? *The Sheik and the Maiden?* Perhaps we could visit a costume shop."

"Perhaps we could," she murmured, lifting her face for his kiss.

A black and green cab pulled up. They broke apart. Jeremy opened the door and slid in after her.

"Two Hundred Ten Crestwood Drive," she said, "and would you mind stopping at an ATM?"

Jeremy leaned back and put his arm around her shoulders. "What's an ATM?"

Sherry flashed him a grin. "It is one of the little differences I told you about. I'll show you."

Jeremy watched the passing traffic. "The cars look different, but I expected more Bubble cars . . . Monorails . . . Flying cars. This is all rather mundane."

She laughed. "Darling, you have an Aston Martin. I don't think they come any better than that."

The driver stopped at a Bank of America. "Come with me," Sherry said.

Jeremy gave an involuntary grunt as he unfolded his long body from the cab.

"What?" Sherry asked.

"I am used to my knees working a bit better," he said, smiling crookedly.

She winced for him. "I take yoga and it helps a lot."

He stretched the kinks out of his shoulders. "When I get home, I'm going to take it up. I had no idea what old could feel like."

"This is an ATM, an Automatic Teller Machine," she explained, sliding her card into the machine. "You put in your password and it gives you cash. No need to wait until the bank is open."

Jeremy's eyes widened as he watched the cash pop out of the slot. "Only in America."

"No. They are everywhere in the world. Most banking and bill paying is done online these days."

"Online." He drew out the word as if it were a title to a film. "Another new term." They got back in the cab. Jeremy winced. "I could do without these twinges."

She leaned over and rubbed his knee. "I am so sorry. We won't stay long."

Jeremy contradicted her. "Yes. We will."

Sherry paid off the driver. The too warm wind swirled up and gusted leaves around them.

Jeremy looked from the blooming profusion of roses in the front yard to the leafy tree shadowing the porch. He sniffed the air. "I smell lemons."

Sherry nodded. "I have orange trees and avocado in the back yard. Also grapefruit and apricot. It's nice being able to pick your own fruit salad." She unlocked the front door and waved him in.

Jeremy looked around at the creamy plaster walls broken by graceful arches. The crystal chandelier cast a golden light over the Hepplewhite dining table. In the living room a cream carpet woven in red and maroon roses shielded the dark hardwood floor. The colors were echoed by the drapes on the French windows.

The huge flat screen dominating one wall stopped him in his tracks. He leaned against the wall and folded his arms. "Do you have your own movie theatre then?"

"No," Sherry laughed, "this is what televisions look like now." She picked up the remote and flicked it on. She switched the channels and stopped at CNN.

Jeremy read the little ticker tape running along the bottom of the screen. "In the news tonight President Barack Obama announced a visit to the troops in Afghanistan." His jaw dropped as a picture displayed on the screen. "America has a black president? I don't believe it."

"You can believe in time travel more easily than you can a black president?"

He thought about that for a moment. "Yes."

Sherry flicked off the TV. "Come on. I have to show you one of my favorite future things." She grabbed his hand and led him to the den.

Built in bookshelves filled two walls floor to ceiling. Jeremy's eyes focused on the Queen Anne desk.

She tried to visualize what he was seeing. The desktop held what looked to be an empty black picture frame on a small silver stand and an egg shaped plastic object on a soft pad. A silver metal case sat underneath the desk. "That's my computer."

Jeremy looked at it in disbelief. "They got that small?"

"There are bigger ones. This is a personal computer." She reached under the desk and turned it on.

There was a whirring and clicking and the melodic sound of the Windows Start Up screen. The black picture frame lit up. She pushed Jeremy into the desk chair. "You are going to love this."

The screen changed to her desktop wallpaper. A shot of her sons at ages five and eight. Jeremy tensed. "Are those your children?"

Damn. She had forgotten about the picture. "Yes. That's John," she said, pointing to the older boy with a mop of brown curly hair. "He was eight in that picture. That's his soccer uniform. This is Michael." The younger boy stood proudly in his Superman costume. His straight brown bangs brushed his eyebrows. "He was five when that was taken."

She reached over Jeremy's shoulder. "This thing is called a mouse. I have no idea why," she said, forestalling his question. "You see that little arrow that is on the screen? You point it at an icon and click on it. She pointed at the Firefox logo and clicked the left mouse button.

Jeremy watched her closely

Her Google page screen came up. "And this is what we call the World Wide Web or the Internet." She motioned to him to take the desk chair. "Type in anything. Ask the computer whatever you want."

"Looks rather like a flat typewriter." Jeremy sat and placed his fingers on the keyboard. "Anything?"

"Ask it what films are playing. Ask it for news. Ask it for a history of cricket."

Sherry dropped a kiss on the top of his head, glad he could not see her eyes. "Ask it what films are playing. Ask it for news. Anything. I don't know. Ask it for a history of cricket."

"Now there's an idea." He typed in 'history of cricket.'

The screen changed and listed a series of sources. On the left hand side of the screen it said *'About 286,000,000 results. (0.24 seconds)'*

Jeremy stared in amazement. "Two hundred and eighty-six million results? That's ridiculous." He clicked on the first article. "What's this *Wikipedia*?"

"It's sort of an encyclopedia created by all the users of the web. Anyone who has knowledge of a subject can type it in, so it's not always reliable. Try another question." Sherry's eyes grew mischievous. "Type in 'what happened in 1984?' We all grew up with that book by George Orwell."

He did. A new list of articles sprung up. "Click on the Wikipedia one," Sherry suggested, leaning over his shoulder.

His eyes widened in shock. "Ye gods! Ronald Reagan did become President. That is beyond bizarre."

She pointed to the little wheel on top of the mouse. "If you stroke that, it will move down the page."

He tried it. "That's very nice. What does it mean when the letters are in blue?"

"That means you can click on those words and it will take you to another place."

He played with the mouse button scrolling up and down. "This is fascinating." His eyes fixed on the box that said '21st century.' "I want to see that." He moved the mouse carefully and clicked on it.

"No," she said, "not yet." She didn't want him reading about the World Trade Center. "Try something more in your line of work. How about two headed alien baby?"

He grinned. "All right." He typed it in. A new page sprang up. "Well, apparently two headed alien babies have not gone out of style."

He looked at the square picture with a triangle on it. "What do I do with this?"

"Oh, that's a YouTube video." She reached over and guided his hand to click on it. The video was very clear. Unsurprisingly the two-headed alien baby was in a test tube.

Sherry explained how to go back to a previous search and watched him experiment.

"I can see where this would be hard to stop." Jeremy tapped and clicked, totally focused on the screen.

"Yes. Do you want a glass of wine or a cola?"

He nodded, still absorbed in his play. "Please." He didn't say which.

On her way to the kitchen, Sherry saw a note propped up against the answering machine. *'Sherry, check your machine. I told Claire we were going to the The Expanding Light in Nevada City. I am going to The Castle to try 1969 Los Angeles. I'll see you when I get back. Love. PS do NOT tell Claire!!'*

Sherry listened to the recorded greeting. Lorena had Sherry's voice down pat. What was she up to? Why on earth would Lorena go to 1969 Los Angeles?

She opened the lone bottle of wine left in the kitchen wine rack and poured them both a glass. As an afterthought, she reached into the fridge for a coke. Jeremy might be in shock. Maybe sugar was a better idea . . .

She handed him the opened Coke. He drank it, not looking up from the computer.

Sherry retrieved the iPhone from her purse and plugged it in. Jeremy didn't look up. Men! True love and new toys were in different compartments in their brains. They couldn't remember both at the same time.

"I'll leave you to find your way about."

He nodded, totally absorbed.

She marveled at the silver in his hair, then touched her own self-consciously. She went to the bathroom mirror and examined her roots. No silver. Well not much anyway. Not enough to worry about.

She checked the bedroom. The covers were tossed back just as she had left them. "Bad housekeeper," she scolded herself. She re-made the bed with fresh sheets and plumped up the pillows and returned to the den. Jeremy had not moved an inch. "Jeremy?"

"Someone shot John Lennon." He turned to her in shock.

"Yes. I am sorry." She sighed at the tragic look on his face. "Look, you cannot take in forty odd years in a night."

She put her hands on his shoulders and dropped a loving kiss on the top of his head. "Give it a rest."

Jeremy's hands dropped from the keyboard. He swiveled the chair, and caught her hands, bringing them to his lips. He examined her fingers and kissed each one.

He looked at his own hands. "It is a very strange feeling, being this old."

Sherry laughed. "Tell me about it. I didn't get old in a night, but it still feels weird. I see my face in a mirror and I wonder who that old lady is." She touched his face. "I know you've aged on the outside, but what about the inside? Now do you feel any older?"

"No. I feel exactly the same."

"Same here. On the inside I feel the same as I did when I was twenty. Only now I've had forty-three more years' experience. I guess that makes me better at being me."

"Maybe that's why you don't feel old to me." Jeremy rose with only a slight wince. He drew her to him and kissed her.

Her lips caught fire. "This is amazing," she whispered against his lips. "I still feel like I did before we came through the door."

His hands cradled the small of her back and drew her tight against him. "I'm delighted to report that all of my parts seem to be in working order." He deepened the kiss.

Sherry could feel the truth of his statement pressing her abdomen. She stood on tiptoe and clasped her arms around his neck, bringing him closer.

They broke gasping for air.

"Come on," he urged "show me your bedroom. I want to see if I like sex with you as much as I did two hours ago."

Sherry nodded wordlessly.

She paused in the bedroom doorway. "Do you mind if we turn out the lights? I am not sure I am ready for you to see all of me in the flesh."

"Whatever you want." Jeremy's brows quirked up. "I'm not ready to see me in the flesh, either." He flicked off the bedroom light and captured her lips.

The familiar heat raced through her like a lit fuse to dynamite. Sherry stopped thinking. She sank down on to the bed, bringing him with her.

He made short work of her clothes. Covering her body with the warmth of his, he explored her with kisses.

Their sighing turned to short gasps.

Sherry unbuttoned his shirt. Fumbled with the buckle on his belt with fingers made clumsy by building urgency.

Jeremy moved her hands, stripped off his clothes swiftly, and resumed his journey down her body with slow, laving kisses.

"Now! Please." Her body ached for the whirling rapture.

"Sherry," he whispered against her lips. He entered her slowly, as if for the first time. Their bodies fused in rich silken splendor. The loving strokes quickened until the pressure became unbearable and her world shattered in explosions of light.

Jeremy eased himself out and rested his head on her shoulder. "What a wonderful surprise," he said dreamily. "I had no idea the equipment would still work this well at my advanced age."

The warm weight of him on top of her felt wonderful. "Oh god, I wish this could go on forever."

"There is always tomorrow." He spooned himself around her "Sleep my love."

She felt her eyes closing. It's not true, she wanted to tell him. We have to go back and you have to stay there. Sleep rolled over her like a cloud.

Chapter 26
Lorena

"You're going to burn," Lorena said, rubbing oil into Dave's back. "I can feel it."

"What's a little sunburn against the joy of the beach?" Dave shaded his eyes with his hands. "Do you see that girl with the red string bikini?"

Lorena pushed him away. "No! And you'd better not be looking either."

I'm not *looking*, looking. I'm thinking." Dave took the oil from her and began massaging it into her shoulders. "I wondered if . . ." his voice trailed off and his fingers stopped moving.

She turned to look at him. He was a thousand miles away wearing his writer's look. Lorena sighed, then reached into her beach bag and offered him a legal pad and pen. "Go ahead. Don't mind me."

Dave blinked and refocused. "I was wishing I'd remembered my notepad. You're going to make a great writer's wife." He dropped an absentminded kiss on her forehead.

"Gee, thanks," she said dryly. "And you're going to make a great Mr. Anderson."

"Huh?"

"At the 2005 Emmy's, they called you Mr. Anderson."

"That's so wrong." He looked away from the girl in the string bikini. Stared out at the ocean and started scribbling.

Lorena rolled over onto her back on the outsized beach towel they shared. Reveling in the heat of the sun, she listened to "Let the Sunshine in" and "Bad Moon Rising" blaring from competing boom boxes.

The last few days had been wonderful.

They walked a lot, looking at the mansions close to where Dave lived and trying to decide which one they would buy after he published his first book. They argued books and politics and ate hot dogs at Pinks and hamburgers at the original Tommy's. They made love endlessly.

Today they'd headed for Santa Monica.

The rhythmic slap of waves and sound of the gulls mixed with the boom boxes and the delighted squeals of children making an odd kind of lullaby. She turned onto her stomach and slipped into a contented haze.

The icy drip of water on her sun warmed back made her squeal in outrage. She flipped over and looked up at a grinning Dave. "You're going to pay for that."

"If you can catch me. Last one in is a rotten egg."

She sprang to her feet and raced him to the water glorying in the feel of her young body.

The sun dipped low in the sky as they tried to get rid of the worst of the sand at the little beach shower. They climbed the steps to the weather-beaten pier. The smell of creosote mingled with the scent of frying fish.

"I'm hungry. Let's eat at The Breaker's," Dave said.

Worn timbers creaked under the weight of hundreds of feet as they strolled through the crowd past tatty souvenir stalls to the end of the pier where several fishermen manned their poles.

"The pier got shortened in the eighties in a bad storm," Lorena said, staring up at the blue and white sign. "This restaurant's not here in the future."

"That's a shame because they make the best clam chowder you've ever tasted." He led her into the cool dim dining room. Wide windows overlooked the water. "At least I get to show you one thing you haven't seen before."

Lorena admitted the superiority of the chowder. She dowsed her French fries with malt vinegar and looked up into Dave's amused eyes. "What?"

"Everything you do is like you're doing it for the first time."

Lorena's heart cracked. Every day with him was the first time and the last time. Five more days before she had to go back.

They stopped at the Hippodrome to visit the Carousel with its hand carved animals and calliope music, Dave bought two twenty-five cent tickets. Lorena chose a flower-bedecked white horse. Dave took the black lion next to it.

Lorena leaned her head back and followed the path of twinkling lights as the brass poles revolved to the tinny sounds of *In the Good Old Summertime*.

The ride gradually slowed and came to a stop. Dave dismounted, giving the lion a lingering pat. "The only thing wrong with this carousel is that there's no brass ring."

"Wrong, boyo." Lorena grabbed his face and kissed him. "You're my brass ring and don't you forget it."

The music changed to *The Carousel Waltz*?"

Dave looked at her and bowed gravely. "Shall we?"

Lorena curtsied and offered him her hand. "We shall."

He took her in his arms. They waltzed around the carousel, gazes locked on each other, oblivious to the revolving lights.

Lorena took her hand off his shoulder and put it around his waist to draw him closer.

Dave shuddered. "I think we'd better head home now." He spun her around to walk in front of him.

Lorena didn't want to wait that long. Her body ached for fulfillment. "How do you feel about car sex?"

He drew a ragged breath. "Right now it's at the top of my list." He hurried her down the steps to the parking lot.

Chapter 27
Sherry

Sherry struggled out of a dream of loss and grief and reached for Jeremy. The space beside her was empty. *No!* Her eyes snapped open and winced at the stab of sunlight. She grabbed her robe and hurried to the den.

Jeremy hunched over the computer wearing his jeans and nothing else. The sight of him chased away the remnants of the dream. Her heart resumed its warm steady beat, but not the rest of her. "It's freezing in here. I'll get your jacket." She went back to the bedroom and put on slippers, wishing she had some for Jeremy. She grabbed his jacket and punched up the heat on the thermostat. A warm dusty smell emanated from the vents.

Jeremy hadn't moved an inch. She looked at the computer screen and her heart froze in remembered pain. The World Trade Center as the plane crashed into the second tower. Sherry put the jacket around his shoulders, hugging him close. "I am so sorry. I hoped you wouldn't find that."

"Are we ever going to stop finding fresh ways to kill each other?" Jeremy muttered, his back rigid.

The first tower crumbled. Sherry put her hand over his on the mouse and turned off the Internet.

Jeremy slumped back in his seat and stared at the keyboard.

A plane buzzed overhead.

Sherry fitted herself into Jeremy's lap, resting her head on his shoulder. "We humans do terrible things sometimes.

But we also do wonderful things like finding new ways to cure each other."

"I don't think the curing is keeping pace with the killing." His arms cradled her loosely. "One good thing. Vietnam is over."

Sherry seized Jeremy's hands and drew him to his feet. "Come away. No more future history."

He winced and put both hands on his back. "This body doesn't seem to like to be in the same position for any length of time."

Jeremy followed her into the sunny kitchen and leaned against the counter, rubbing the small of his back. "It wasn't all bad news. I looked up discoveries in molecular research. It made me want to go back to the lab and be a part of it again. There's a string theory that . . ." He broke off and watched Sherry grind the beans for coffee and fill a carafe with water. "Is that a tiny Cappuccino machine?"

"Yup." Sherry opened the fridge and grabbed the milk. She opened the freezer. "I'll nuke us a couple of breakfast quiche."

"You'll what?"

Sherry giggled at the horrified look on his face. "Nuke." She pointed to the large white metal box on the counter. "This is a microwave oven. It uses an energy wave to heat food up fast."

Jeremy walked over to it and opened and closed the door several times. "Radiation shielded, I presume?"

"I used to be afraid it wasn't," she admitted. "When I got my first microwave, I was afraid to heat the baby's bottle in it. I kept thinking, what if this turns out to be one of those inventions where they tell you twenty years later that you've killed your child?"

Jeremy's eyes shadowed at the word baby. "Can I see some more pictures of your children?"

Sherry's heart contracted. "Of course. I'll be right back." She returned with two large scrapbooks. "This is Michael's and this is John's."

Jeremy opened the first album and flicked through pictures of Sherry holding a baby and then, a toddler. The next picture showed a tall fair-haired man with one arm around Sherry and his other arm around the boy. Jeremy's hands white knuckled on the page.

"That's Bill." Sherry didn't know what to say. Her hands moved to Jeremy's shoulders and kneaded a soothing rhythm. "I can't change it. I didn't know you. Knowing you now, a part of me wishes they were yours. But only a part of me, because I love them exactly the way they are."

Jeremy continued to study the picture. "Tell me about Bill . . . about your marriage."

Sherry sighed. "I met Bill right before I turned thirty. My biological clock had started to sound like Big Ben." She looked unseeingly out to the patio. "We liked a lot of the same things—books, movies. We made each other laugh. I thought that was important. When he proposed, I accepted. I thought I was in love."

She shook her head in wonderment. How could she have thought the feelings of friendship, and contentment she'd shared with Bill were real love? They had nothing to do with the dazzling earth-shattering wave of emotion she felt every time she looked at Jeremy and found the center of her world.

Jeremy waited for her to continue.

"I expected Bill and I would be together forever. When he began to grow distant and unavailable, I blamed pressures at work." Sherry's fingers tightened on Jeremy's shoulders. "The pressure at work turned out to be the new head of HR. Brittany Wells. Fresh out of college. Candy floss hair, baby doll eyes, and a figure to die for."

Jeremy reached around and patted her bottom. "Your figure is perfection. I don't see how she competed."

Sherry swatted his hand away. "Hey, this is my life drama. Don't distract me. We got a civilized divorce and I refrained from pulling out Brittany's candy floss blonde hair by its dark roots."

"Why?"

"Two reasons, John and Michael. I didn't mind losing Bill nearly as much as I minded the boys losing Bill. They were already wounded by our separation. I wasn't going to add to their pain by feuding with Bill's new wife." Her fingers continued the pressure down Jeremy's spine. "We've done well with it. We're so civilized that that Brittany invited me to dinner for my birthday last week."

She smiled at Jeremy's look of disbelief. "I didn't go. I went on a Virtual Reality adventure instead." She bent down and pressed her cheek to his. "The best thing that ever happened to me," she whispered.

The espresso machine hissed. She turned away to steam the milk for the cappuccinos and nuke the quiche.

Jeremy continued to turn pages. "Is this the home wrecker?"

Sherry turned to see what he was looking at. John in a black cap and gown. An older Sherry stood beside him. Bill had one arm around John and the other round a pretty blonde woman. A blonde pre-teen sporting a mouth full of braces stood next to her smiling self-consciously. "Yes. That's Bill and Brittany and their daughter Carrie."

The microwave dinged. She pulled out the plate and set it next to him. "Watch out, it's hot," she warned.

"Bill must have been off his rocker. She hasn't half your charm." He reached for the quiche and yelped as it burned him.

"Well, I told you it was hot." Sherry handed him a foam topped coffee cup. "Try the cappuccino."

Jeremy took a cautious sip. "This is good."

"Yup. Brits don't understand coffee. We do it better."
Sherry absently stirred her cappuccino. "Maybe Brittany
is Bill's soul mate. They've done twenty-three good years
together. I can appreciate that more now that I know what
a soul mate feels like." She looked up at Jeremy. His eyes
mirrored her pain.

Jeremy reached for her and pulled her into his lap. "What
are we going to do, my love?" He buried his face in her hair.

"Nothing." She held him tightly. "There is nothing we
can do."

The kitchen clock ticked out the silence.

"I could stay," Jeremy offered.

"And miss the next forty-three years of your life? No."

He trailed a path of kisses down to her neck. "I want a
world with you in it. That's the important thing."

"Jeremy, you'd lose your family and your work and
everything that is supposed to happen to you. I don't know
what you've done in the past, but I know you probably did
a lot." She took a deep breath and forced a smile. "You'll
probably forget about me. Hearts mend. I know this."

"The chance of forgetting you is right up there with
forgetting my own name." Jeremy shot her a wicked grin. "Of
course that could be fairly soon considering our advanced
age. How long, do you think, before we become dear dotty
things?"

Sherry put a finger over his lips. "Bite your tongue! I
intend to be functioning intelligently at a hundred and four. I
don't have any plans for dear and dotty."

"Well then, there's no problem. I've got lots of time
left." Jeremy rubbed his chin, grimacing at the stubble. "I
need a shower before we go exploring."

She reached up and stroked his roughened face. "I like
it. Do you know that at some point in the eighties, stubble
will become a fashion statement?"

Jeremy looked skeptical. "Now you are putting me on."

He started toward the bedroom. "I learned a new phrase this morning. Green Conscious." He turned and leered at her invitingly. "Let's be green conscious and save water. We'll shower together."

She laughed. "Did you get any sleep last night?"

"Not much," he admitted. "The Internet is a miracle."

"Well, I'm all for saving the environment." Sherry slid open the shower curtain, adjusted the water and unbelted her robe. She took a deep breath and turned to him. "Sixty three looks a lot different than twenty." She waited for his assessment, conscious of the effects of gravity on her breasts and of the stretch marks crisscrossing her still firm stomach. No amount of exercise had rid her of a slight sagging in her upper arms.

He pulled off his sweater and jeans. His clean lines had blurred. His stomach was softer, his muscles less defined. His body hair shone silver. She still wanted every inch of him.

They looked at each other in the harsh light of morning. He reached and took her into his arms. "Nothing important changed," he murmured. He lifted her with him into the shower and closed the curtain.

Chapter 28
Lorena

"Disneyland?" Lorena looked at him incredulously. "You're kidding, right?"

Tonight they were back at C.C. Brown's Ice Cream Parlor. Since that first night Lorena had thought of it as *their place.*"

Dave ran his spoon around the brown china pitcher to get the last drops of hot fudge sauce. "This is your first visit to Los Angeles. You have to go to Disneyland. I think it's a law or something."

"Disneyland's awfully pricey." Lorena thought of her dwindling pile of travelers' checks. "I'm not sure we can afford it?"

"I'll splurge." Dave reached for her pitcher of hot fudge. "I admit seven-fifty is pretty high, but you're worth it."

"Seven-fifty a ticket? That's it? Wow! Times do change. Okay, let's do it."

Lorena grabbed Dave's hand. "Don't let go! I feel like we're in an episode of *The Twilight Zone.* Main Street looks exactly the way it did when I visited with Claire, Jeff, and Dylan a couple of months ago. Surely something should be different."

Dave grinned down at her "The time traveler thinks she's in the Twilight Zone? Imagine that!" He lowered his voice to a portentous rumble. "*You are traveling through another dimension, a dimension not only of sight and sound but of mind. A journey into a wondrous land of imagination."*

They finished it together. *"Next stop, the Twilight Zone!"*

"Funny." Dave grinned. "That sounds like something Disney should have written."

Lorena scanned the window of the Main Street Emporium. "Look! They're selling framed celluloids from the original *Peter Pan* and they're only two dollars! I want some."

Dave turned Lorena away from the window. "Later. I don't want to carry stuff. Come on. They opened a new attraction called the Tiki Room. I haven't seen it yet."

Hands clasped, they wandered toward Adventure Land.

Dave loved the talking birds and wouldn't stop humming the song. Lorena bought him a Dole Whip in self-defense. They sailed on the Jungle Boat Cruise, clambered up The Swiss Family Tree House and voyaged with the Pirates of the Caribbean. Twice.

"I'm starving," Dave said. "Let's eat."

A smiling hostess led them into the cool recesses of the Blue Bayou.

"I love this place," Lorena said, looking around at the star-studded night sky. The dining area was hung with lanterns. A woman in a crinoline dress stood on the balcony of the Southern plantation playing a violin. Faintly in the background she could hear the screams as people hit the first water slide. "It's the only place in the world you can dine to violins and screams."

"How come we have to meet in Mackinac?" Dave wondered aloud. "It would be a lot more fun to propose to you here."

Lorena caught her breath. "Yes it would, but that isn't the way it happened."

"Let's make it happen." Dave took her hand. He moved his chair aside and got down on one knee.

"David! Stop it." Lorena's face flamed. "People are looking at us."

"Let them look. Lorena Anderson, I love you to the depth and breadth of my soul and I want to spend the rest of my life doing that. Will you marry me?"

Lorena looked around. People were definitely staring. "Yes. Now get up."

"Come on." He kissed her hand. "You can do better than that."

Lorena's heart swelled. She reached down and framed his beautiful, expectant face with her hands. "David Cramer I will love you my whole life without fail. I will honor you and cherish you, but I promise," she lifted an eyebrow, "I will not always obey you. Get up you fool."

He reached into his pocket and removed a ring.

She stared open mouthed at the golden circlet with its five pearls surrounded by chip diamonds. Her ring. The one she'd left in the future. Lorena snatched her hand back. "Where did you get that ring?"

"I've always had it. My grandmother left it to me. She called it a princess ring." He looked unsure. "Do you mind having a second hand ring? I can get you something else if you don't like it."

Past and present rolled together in her mind. They were changing things. What were they doing to their shared future? She shoved the thoughts away. Too late to worry. We've already done it.

She smiled tremulously and held out her hand to Dave. "It's not second hand. It's a family ring and it's perfect."

He fitted it on to her left hand and kissed it into place.

A smattering of applause sounded from their fellow diners. The violinist on the balcony started playing the "Wedding March." A beaming server brought slices of cake and the specialty Mint Julep. They smiled and accepted congratulations.

"You planned this," Lorena accused, unbearably moved and not wanting to show it with everyone looking at them.

"Yes, my love, I did. I don't know that your time here is limited, because I am going to do everything I can to change that, but I want to know right now that you are mine. Only mine."

"But I am. You were, are, my first and only love and always will be." She blinked back tears. "Hey, when you get it right the first time there is nothing to change."

"I am going to try to keep you here." He turned his hand up into hers and squeezed it. "I don't see why we can't fight time. How do you feel about living your life over again, maybe just a little differently?"

"Dave, I've read one time travel book in my whole life and the only thing that stuck in my head is that you're not supposed to change the past." She reached across the table and traced his smile with a loving finger. "We've already changed things. I don't know if I can stay, but I would gladly live over every day of my life including Junior High school."

Dave covered his eyes. "Please, not Junior High."

"If I could live it with you."

"Then we're going to defy time." He pulled her to her feet, tossed ten dollars on the table to cover their bill, and ushered her to the exit. "Do you want to call your family?"

"No." Lorena froze. "David, I know this is stupid, but I only now realized something. I am alive twice in this time right now."

David stopped. "You're right. I didn't think about that. Where is the other you? How do you know she is there?"

"At home in Ohio. I remember because I watched the moon landing with my family."

Dave didn't say anything. They walked back out into the hot sunlight toward the Haunted Mansion.

"Oh," Lorena said, disappointed, "it's not open yet."

"No. Rumor has it that the mansion is really haunted and that's why it's taking so long to open. Now they are saying it will open in August." David stared at the mansion with a frown on his face. "You don't know for sure that you're in Ohio. You could call and find out. Maybe our future is already changed."

Lorena stopped in her tracks, frozen by the thought of changed time for her other ghost-like self. "What if we don't get married? What if we had a terrible fight, and what if you found someone else? And what if . . ."

"The moon was made of green cheese?" David interrupted, laughing. "Listen, we don't understand time and space. Someone said time is a game we made up to keep everything from happening all at once."

He walked her to a shaded bench and sat down. Lorena snuggled into his shoulder.

Dave picked up her hand and shifted it so the sunlight played on her ring. "Some things are beyond time. When I saw you in Schwab's that first day, something changed. You were a lodestone pulling me. Now I know why. You were born so I could love you. I was born so you could love me. Nothing will change that."

She sighed and gripped his hand as if they were a lifeline. Shouts echoed from two canoes racing the river. The Mark Twain steamed by majestically and blew its whistle.

Dave was silent. She could tell he was hunting for words. "Did you ever throw a stone in still water?"

She nodded.

"The ripples go out from that stone in widening circles. The stone's throw changes the surface of the water. But the water doesn't change. Eventually the ripples die off and the surface is still again. It goes on." Dave looked at her. "I think you coming here might be a stone in the water. Things have changed, but in another way they haven't."

She considered his words. "You know what would be wonderful? If you didn't die. If I went back to the future and you were there waiting for me. If the ripple of this act could give us one thing, I would want it to be that."

"Oh, Lorena." He sighed and automatically reached for his pack of cigarettes.

She saw the desire in his face. "They sell cigarettes at the smoke shop on Main Street." She was *not* going to nag about it. He had to make his own decision. "You could get another pack."

"No." Dave shook his head. "This will pass. Come on, let's walk. That will help."

They strolled toward the Country Bear Jamboree. "I still think you should call your home. Or I could do it for you?"

"All right," she said, resigned. "You do it."

"When we get back to the apartment," he promised. "If you're not there, only one of you exists." He squeezed her hand. "And I'm going to marry that one in December."

Lorena didn't believe it. She remembered the face of the ticket. Void after two weeks. "If I changed time, we will be married next April." She stood on tiptoe and brought his face down to kissing level. "I am planning a hell of a big wedding."

Dave groaned.

Chapter 29
Sherry

The strains of "Zip-a-Dee-Doo-Dah" came from the den. "That's John. I know by the ring." Sherry tugged her sweater down over her head and dashed for the den.

Jeremy followed, shirt in hand.

Sherry grabbed her iPhone and disengaged it from the base. "Hi, John, how are you?" She listened to the excited voice on the other end, her eyes wide with wonder. "The sonogram shows twins! I can't believe it. How's Janie feeling?" Her face fell. "Well of course you have to spend Thanksgiving with them. I understand."

Jeremy slipped an arm around her and leaned her back against him.

She turned to look up at Jeremy. "John, someone's at the door. I have to go. I'll call you on Thanksgiving. Love you!" She clicked end.

Jeremy reached for the phone and studied the icons on the screen.

Sherry took it back and tapped the pictures icon. She flipped through the images until she came to a picture of John and Janie's wedding. They looked so happy and in love. She stroked the picture and made it into a close-up. "This is John and Janie's wedding picture."

"How did you do that? Make it big?"

She showed him.

He took the phone from her and played with the picture zooming in and out. "Fascinating" he remarked.

"Yes."

"So you are going to be a grandmother. Congratulations. I think." His hands shook as he handed the phone back to her. "I am having a difficult time with all this."

Sherry looked at him. His lips were blue tinged. She eased him down into the desk chair.

"Don't know what's wrong." He breathed in short heavy gasps. "Can't seem to catch my breath."

She felt his pulse. Jackhammer fast. "I'm going to call my doctor."

"No!" Jeremy concentrated on taking deeper breaths.

Sherry felt his pulse slow.

"I'm all right. Don't call anyone." He gave her a tiny smile. "I didn't bring my passport. They'll throw me in jail."

Sherry kept her hand on his wrist. His color looked better. "I can't tell whether you had a panic attack or a mild heart attack." She knew which one she was having. She was terrified.

Jeremy looked revolted. "Men do not have panic attacks." He thought for a moment. "It must have been the quiche."

"You didn't eat the quiche," she reminded him. Her heart raced. The obvious answer occurred to her. "Jeremy, what do you think happens to your system when you age forty-three years in a single moment?"

The realization hit him. "Oh. Probably nothing good."

"We need to go back."

Jeremy rubbed his chest. "But I haven't seen anything yet. I . . ."

"Right now," Sherry ordered. "I'll get the car."

Jeremy looked as if he wanted to argue.

Sherry stared him down.

"All right. I would like to spend a bit more time on the computer though."

"No! You've seen enough." She tried to smile. "I will bet *Twenty-Eight* is going to be carrying some very peculiar stories in the next few years."

"It already does, my love. And I wouldn't take that bet." Sherry grabbed her purse and their jackets and hurried him out the door.

Jeremy looked at the Prius sitting in the driveway with interest. "I'll drive," he offered.

"Nope," Sherry said. "I don't think we will have your first lesson on driving on the right hand side today. Besides, I know where we are going."

Jeremy opened the door for her and helped her into the driver's seat. "Bet I could do it," he muttered.

"I am sure you could," Sherry agreed, not wanting to upset him any further, "but not today. I want to get you back in one piece."

Jeremy folded himself into the passenger seat and yawned. "Wake me when we get there." His eyes drooped shut.

The drive to Burbank was swift in the light Sunday traffic. Sherry parked the car in The Castle's self-park. She shook Jeremy gently. "We're here."

His eyes blinked open to the sight of The Castle in daylight. "Very impressive." He sounded sleep dazed. He flinched as he swung his legs to the pavement. "I'm going into training," he muttered. "If the astronauts can do it, so can I. It's simply a matter of will power. I'm coming back here with you."

"We'll talk about it later," she soothed. She put an arm around his waist and guided his steps to the entrance.

Sherry smiled at the Maître d' as he hurried forward. "We're here for the VR adventure. I know my way back."

He nodded and stepped aside.

Jeremy's eyes lit up at the sound of the grinding thrum. "Now that's what computers sound like in my day." He disengaged himself from her arm and limped to the desk. "Good afternoon. I'm with *Twenty-Eight*, a London magazine and I'd love a tour of your computer set up. Could you tell me how all this works?"

"Jeremy," Sherry said sharply, "we need to go."

Eric put down his phone and blinked up at Jeremy, a confused look on his face. "Sorry, Sir, I'm not allowed to admit anyone to the computer room. You'd have to talk to management about that. Can I help you with anything else?"

Jeremy scanned the large menu posted on the wall. "Have you ever taken one of these adventures yourself? What's it like?"

Eric's eyes lit up. "They're awesome. I programmed my girlfriend and me to the first surfing championship in Hawaii. Christmas," he elaborated, "1954. It was wicked, dude. Ah . . . Sir. You really feel like you're in another time." He grinned at Jeremy. "I'm saving up to take her to Paris in 1921. She likes old school dancing. We're taking lessons."

"That sounds very tempting." Jeremy swung around to Sherry, keeping a hand on the desk for balance. His eyes filled with mischief. "How do you feel about Paris in 1921?"

Sherry gritted her teeth and tried to look casual. "No thanks, love. I've got my heart set on 1969." She handed Eric her credit card. "We'd like to go to London."

Jeremy craned his neck trying to see what Eric was punching in.

The set of Jeremy's lips told her it was all he could do to stand upright. "Idiot," she whispered, "what are you playing at?"

"I want to see how it works." He watched attentively as the white box attached to the computer spit out two plastic cards and a sheaf of check-sized papers. "Those look a bit like the punch cards used to program computers in my time."

Eric looked up startled. "Your time?"

"He means back when he was young. A *long* time ago." She removed Jeremy's hand from the desk and draped it around her shoulders. "Let's go."

Jeremy gave Eric a *Women. What can you do?* look and allowed Sherry to guide him down the hall.

She inserted their tickets and held her breath until the blue light traveled down their bodies. She let it out with a grateful gasp as Jeremy straightened.

He dropped a kiss on top of her head. "The pain's gone." His voice sounded vigorous. He opened the outer door and rain sheeted in. "Marvelous. We'll have to make a run for it."

Using their jackets as shields, they splashed their way back to the Aston Martin. Jeremy turned the heater on full blast. "Home, I think."

Sherry nodded. She could not stop shivering.

They hung their sodden coats on the coat tree. Jeremy went to the living room and switched on the fire. Sherry ran upstairs and changed into jeans and Jeremy's fisherman sweater and a pair of his thickest socks. She rubbed a towel over her head and finger combed her hair without bothering to look in the mirror. Right at this moment she didn't care.

Jeremy passed her on the way down. "I've put on the tea water. Be a dear and make some toast."

She nodded mutely. The kettle sang. She made the tea and toast and carried it into the living room.

Jeremy put a record on the Stereo. He'd changed into cords and fisherman sweater. His hair curled damply from the rain. "It doesn't get any better than this. Verdi, the Sunday Times, tea, toast, and of course," he said with a lurking smile, "you."

She sat on the sofa and poured the tea.

He took a cup and a piece of toast. He opened the paper.

"Do you like crosswords? We could do it together."

Sherry tried to sound like her heart wasn't cracking. "I love them but I don't understand English cluing. I tried one when I lived here before and it didn't make any sense to me."

"Never mind," he said lazily. He put the paper down and pulled her to him. "I don't feel like reading the paper. I'd rather sit here with you and listen to the music."

"Yes" she murmured. She snuggled in to his warmth. She could feel his heartbeat. Verdi's "The Four Seasons" made a lovely background to the snapping of the fire.

"I read up on time travel last night."

Sherry's head snapped up. "You what?"

"In your day, physicists had discovered the math that makes time travel possible. It's the *how* they can't agree on." He curled a lock of her hair around his finger. "I'm sure of one thing. That VR nonsense is a cover up. Someone made a time machine and didn't want anyone to know."

Sherry nodded. "I figured that much out for myself."

"Here's the good part." He sat her up and turned her to face him. "I read a number of hypotheses about what could happen if one time traveled. One theory is that if we do travel back in time, we set up an infinite number of probabilities. In one probability you could stay with me and live happily ever after. And that probability wouldn't erase the time track where you married Bill and had two children. Think of them as alternate dimensions."

Sherry felt joy so deep it felt like pain. Then she shook her head. "It's a theory. I can't risk them on a theory. I would never know whether or not I had killed them."

"Another theory is time protection. This postulates that it's impossible for you to go back and change history so that your children would be unborn because time itself would prevent it."

"And how would time do that?" she asked, skeptically.

"Probably by having you fall out of love with me and go

back to America and marry Bill."

Sherry frowned. "I don't like that theory at all."

"Nor do I." Jeremy's lips firmed. "I am going to find a way to make this work for us if I have to invent the damned machine myself."

"That would be wonderful." She gave him a watery smile. "If you invent it maybe you could make it so I could stay a little longer." She drew a tiny breath and let it out. "I have to go back. If I stay much longer I'll become a missing person. I can't do that to my children."

He settled her back into his arms. "When you go back, I'm coming with you. I only need a bit of time to put things right here."

"No! It's too hard on your body. The next trip could kill you. Wait." Jeremy's words played back in her mind. *A bit of time to put things right . . .* She clutched his hand. "What's to keep me from going forward and getting a new ticket to come back? I could put things right at home. Come up with a story for Michael and John. Arrange for Adele to hire extra help for the store and come back for another week with you."

"You could tell them you are going on a buying trip to London. That should work." He yawned. "One thing I've learned, knowing you will age, and feeling it, are two different things entirely."

"Yes," she murmured. "They are." She could feel his body grow heavy against hers.

"Tomorrow I'm going to join a gym. Start getting . . ." His voice trailed off into sleep.

Sherry concentrated on memorizing the feel of his body against hers, his scent, and the light tickle of his breath against her cheek. She brushed her tears away and cradled him close.

Chapter 30
Lorena

"Sorry. Wrong number." Dave hung up the phone. "Dammit, you're there. I'd know your voice anywhere."

"I was afraid it would work that way." Lorena slumped back on the battered sofa. "I kept hoping the old me would have winked out of existence. I really wanted to stay."

"How much more time?" He reached for his nonexistent pack of cigarettes and remembered.

"Two days." Lorena watched him thoughtfully. "You know if you stay quit, I may never take up smoking. That will be weird."

"Wait a minute. You smoked?"

"Yes. I started after Claire was born."

He gave her an incredulous look.

"Well," she said defensively, "you were doing it. And it felt companionable. I got used to it."

"But you quit when I got cancer, didn't you? You don't smoke anymore?"

Lorena stared at the cracked wall. "I smoked more than ever after you died."

"Why," Dave asked. He looked bewildered.

"I couldn't kill myself directly." She crossed her arms on her chest to keep the remembered pain from spilling out. "That wouldn't have been fair to Claire and Jeff and the baby. But I think I thought if I kept smoking, I would join you sooner."

Dave's voice roughened. "That may be the stupidest excuse I ever heard. Listen to me, Lorena. You are never going to smoke. I am personally going to see to it."

"Okay." She moved over and snuggled in to him. "I don't miss it in this body because I haven't started yet. So if I never start, it will be a moot point."

The black and white TV sputtering in the background was tuned to the Apollo mission. Lorena turned it off. "They're filling air space. They won't start the landing until tomorrow."

"You know, we had better make the most of tonight." David wove his fingers through her hair. "Tomorrow we're going to be glued to this set."

"It feels a little weird knowing I am in two places at one time." She reached for his hand and twined her fingers through his, reveling in his closeness. "I am going to have a parallel set of memories."

"Probably. But you won't have them until you go back to the future and you'll be old. Everyone knows old people are crazy, so it won't matter." Dave ducked her punch and pulled her to her feet. "Let's go to the Mayfair and stock up on food." He kissed the tip of her nose. "I'd like to do something special tonight, but I'm broke. Teaching assistants are underpaid."

"So are associate professors." Lorena grinned. "Wait until you see our first house."

Dave smiled down at her. "There is this place you can hike to above the Hollywood Bowl. We could take a picnic and listen to the concert from there. You get a great view."

"Sounds good," Lorena said. "Let's go stock up."

"You were right. The climb was worth it." Lorena sliced some more cheese and added it to her giant sandwich creation. "It changes your perspective, looking down at all those ant people."

"You're out of shape," David commented. "You whined all the way up here."

Lorena narrowed her eyes. "My shape is perfect. I can kick your butt in Karate. I simply hate hills."

"Peace." Dave handed her a glass of wine. "I should never have criticized the cook."

They lay back and looked at the stars while the strains of Stravinsky's "The Rite of Spring" drifted up to them.

Two more days . . .

At 1:18 PM Neil Armstrong had announced that 'The Eagle has landed'. That was six hours ago. The time had been filled with news trivia and speculation, broken by commercials for Brillo Scouring Pads and Tang, *The Astronauts' Drink*.

They filled the time with a cutthroat game of double solitaire.

Lorena played her last card with a flourish. "You owe me two hundred dollars. Dave, you are such a sucker."

Dave glanced at the TV and went into full alert. "Look! The Eagle's door is opening."

They watched together in awed silence as Neil Armstrong started down the ladder.

"You know, this is a miracle," Dave whispered. "I mean we are hearing them all the way from the moon."

Neil Armstrong's mike crackled, making it hard to make out the words. *"That's one small step for man, one giant leap for mankind."*

Lorena reached for David's hand. It felt amazingly poignant to be reliving this and sharing it with David. The solitaire game lay forgotten. They stared, entranced with the small blurry figure on the screen.

Lorena's purse started buzzing. She picked it up and reached inside, her eyes still on the TV, and found the vibrating iPhone. She looked at it in shock. "It's working. How is that possible?"

Dave took it from her. "Weird. I feel it buzzing." The screen lit up. "I think you got a message from the future." He handed it back to her.

The red lettered message flashed over and over. *Ticket expires 20/07/1969 11:59PM. Return to gate."*

"But it hasn't been two weeks," Lorena said, her heart tripping like a jackhammer. "I got here on the seventh."

"It's been two weeks, if you count the first day you were here." Dave looked ready to commit murder. "Throw the damned thing through the window. Screw the future."

Lorena turned the phone off. It turned back on and started buzzing.

"That thing's worse than an alarm clock."

"It *is* an alarm clock. That's one of the features of a cell phone. The alarm will turn itself on even if the phone is turned off." Lorena tapped and fiddled with the screen. "But I didn't set this alarm and I can't find out how to stop it."

"I can." Dave grabbed the phone from her, stalked into the kitchen, pulled a hammer from the drawer, and brought it down hard on the glass. The buzzing stopped. He picked up the pieces and tossed them in the garbage.

Lorena's mouth dropped open. "Dave, you killed an iPhone."

"Damn right. We can't have a piece of the future hanging around in 1969."

Lorena shivered. "That isn't going to make it go away. Dave, I have to go back."

"No you don't." Dave lifted her to her feet. "Stay with me. Let the other you fade away."

"I can't." How many times could a heart break? "What about Claire?"

She saw the doubt in his eyes. His chin firmed. "It's very simple. You live with me for the next three years. In 1972 we'll get married and have Claire." He grinned down at her. "You're a list maker. I'm betting you know the exact date you conceived."

"Of course I do, but . . ."

Dave put his arms around her. "It will work out right. You'll see," he whispered against her lips.

She couldn't think with his arms around her. Reason fought a brief battle with desire. And lost. "I'll stay."

"Yes!" Dave picked her up and whirled her around in a circle.

Lorena wavered between euphoria and terror. She curved her arms around his neck and brought his lips down to meet hers. "I don't know how I thought I could leave."

Dave parked the car at a lot on Selma. "You're serious about this? A job at the Broadway?"

"We have to eat," she reminded him, "and they're hiring."

"I'm trying to imagine you selling clothes."

"Hey, it's a high end store and I'll be a great saleslady. In a month I'll be running the department."

They strolled toward Hollywood Boulevard. The Beach Boys' "Do You Wanna Dance" blasted from a passing car. The smell of pot wafted from three young hippies homesteading against the building.

Lorena pointed at the Taft building. "That's where I came through the door."

David's hand gripped hers tightly. "Just to be safe, let's not cross over there."

"All right." She stopped in front of the door to the Broadway. "You want to wait for me at Aldo's?"

"No. I'll walk over to McCadden's Bookstore. Meet me there and I'll buy you a book."

Lorena rose to her tiptoes and kissed him "I won't be too long." She pushed through the glass revolving door. And found herself in a familiar dimly lit room.

She whirled around. The glass revolving door leading to Hollywood Boulevard was gone. "No!" She slammed her fists against the new door. It didn't budge. The blue light crackled as it traveled down her body. The second door swung open. The Castle hall stretched before her.

Her whole body shook uncontrollably. She slumped back against the door. "I didn't get to say goodbye," she whispered.

Her chin came up. "I won't let it end this way." She strode through the hall to the desk. Eric was back on duty. She smiled at him stiffly. "Hi. I want to go to Los Angeles in 1969. July twenty-first." She fumbled through her purse for her wallet.

Eric grinned at her. "Sure, Marley. Oh, sorry. I mean Ms. Anderson." His fingers hit the keys. "This VR's like, addictive, isn't it?" He frowned at the screen. "Something's out of whack." His fingers played a sonata on the keyboard. He shook his head, puzzled. "I'm real sorry, Ms. Anderson. I can't program it. Looks like Los Angeles 1969 is closed for repairs. Is there anywhere else you'd like to try?"

"No. No, thank you." She turned and walked blindly from the room. She walked through the hall, holding herself erect, braced against the waves of anger and grief washing over her. "You were wrong, Dave," she whispered. "The future's bigger than both of us."

The maître d' smiled at her. "Good to see you, Miss Anderson. How was the adventure?"

Lorena lifted her chin and summoned a smile. "It was more than I ever hoped for."

She made her way to the car. She could feel her age now. "You have the memory," she admonished herself. "You had two more weeks." She clenched her jaw to stop it from trembling. She would cry when she got home.

She reached into the glove compartment for her cigarettes. They weren't there. Did I smoke them all? She waited for the nervous sensation that said she had to have a cigarette right now. It didn't come. She started the car and drove slowly, her mind on automatic pilot.

Chapter 31
Sherry

"I don't want to let you go alone." Jeremy loomed over her holding a protecting black umbrella.

"I'll be fine. I'll get my return ticket right away." Sherry inserted the ticket in the slot and thrust her suitcase into the hall. Her stomach zoomed past her feet. She turned to Jeremy and wrapped her arms around him. The warmth of his kiss spread from her rain cold lips past her rapidly beating heart and settled in her core. "It will be all right," she whispered, as much for herself as for him.

He smiled down at her, eyes wet with something more than rain. "I will love you forever, Sherry Southerland. Hurry back to me."

"I will." She stepped into the small hall and turned round for one last look. The door swung shut. "Wait." She tried to open it. The handle wouldn't budge. Blue light lit the room and the world jolted. The second door swung open.

Sherry hurried down the hall to the desk, her mind busily planning the next two days. Settle things at the store. Adele would flip over the clothes she brought back. Call Michael. Call Lorena. She smiled at a new thought. Get Jeremy a gift from the future. Perhaps a solar powered laptop.

A girl with purple streaked hair sat behind the computer desk, nodding rhythmically to a tune playing on her ear buds.

Sherry tapped on the desk to attract her attention.

The girl removed her ear buds. "Can I help you?"

Sherry beamed at down at her. "I'd like a ticket please. London 1969."

The girl shook her head. "Sorry. Some kind of glitch showed up in the game. All of 1969 is closed for repairs. Is there anywhere else you'd like to go?"

The girl's voice seemed to be coming from an echoing distance. Sherry's mind and body felt old, cracked, and dried. What was it Jeremy had said? *Time protects itself.* Time wasn't going to let her go back.

"Miss, are you all right."

"Yes. I'm fine," she said in a small polite voice. "Thank you." She picked up her suitcase and walked away.

Sherry laid her head on the steering wheel. The Santa Ana winds whipped leaves and empty paper bags against her windshield. "Don't think," she whispered. Putting her key in the ignition, she drove home through almost empty streets, concentrating on the road, ignoring the pain waiting to be dealt with.

The air in her house felt stale and empty. Jeremy's uneaten quiche still sat on the table next to their half filled coffee cups. Tears pooled in her eyes.

She made her way blindly to her bedroom and sat on the bed, reaching for Jeremy's pillow. She held it close, inhaling the trace of his spicy scent. How long before even that disappeared?

She closed her eyes. She saw him smiling at her though the rain. His words echoed in her mind. *I will love you forever. Hurry back to me.*

He's going to think I didn't care enough to come. She cried herself to sleep.

Chapter 32
Lorena

Lorena turned the key in her front door. It was unlocked. How many times do I have to remind myself . . . She pushed the door open and froze. The air smelt different. No stale odor of cigarettes. Maybe Claire came over and cleaned the house?

"Lorena, is that you?"

Time blurred. She was hearing things.

Dave stood in the living room doorway looking the way he looked four years ago, only better. His gray hair was a little shorter, his face tanned and healthy. Lorena sagged against the doorknob.

He strode over and caught her in his arms. "It's all right."

"But you died."

"No," he said, burying his face in her hair. "No, I didn't. You changed all that." He led her into the living room.

The room didn't look the same. Their wedding picture was back on the mantelpiece. The picture of her with Dylan was now a picture of her and Dave with Dylan. Dave's Hugo award which she'd last seen on Claire and Jeff's mantelpiece was back on the bookshelf. "I don't understand." Lorena clutched his hands as if she would never let him go. "When I left to go back to 1969 you were dead in this time."

"I know." Dave looked at her anxiously. "You remember now? Going back to 1969?"

She nodded, her throat too choked to speak.

"Thank God! These last two weeks have been hell. I wasn't sure what you'd remember."

Lorena's head whirled. She couldn't get her mind around it. "I remember you dying. I remember the last four years without you. And now you aren't dead?"

"If you'd ever read any of those time travel books I shoveled at you in the last thirty odd years, you'd know what happened. But you never showed any interest in them." Dave smiled at her. "I'm babbling. Aren't I? The effect of relief." He cupped his hand around the nape of her neck. "Damn, it feels like you've been gone a lifetime." He claimed her lips in a hard hungry kiss.

She wrapped her arms around his neck to draw him closer. The warm solid reality of him pierced the fog of confusion in her mind. She broke the kiss to look up at him. "I don't understand what you're talking about, and I don't care. You're here and that's enough for now."

Dave's arms tightened around her. "I tried so many times to tell you about our first meeting, but something always stopped me. I think time has a way of protecting itself. You couldn't understand too much about time travel, or when you went back, things might have played out differently."

Lorena reached up to stroke his hair. "If this turns out to be a dream, don't wake me."

"It's not a dream, my love." Dave sat down in his recliner and pulled her into his lap. "The future stretches to infinity, but there are possible forks in the road. When you stopped my smoking, you changed our time track. In this future I never died. But this future hinged on you making the trip back to 1969. That had to happen."

She rested her head against his shoulder and closed her eyes. Memories swirled about her in a vortex. Memories of his death and funeral receded and a new set took their place. She saw them at Dylan's third birthday; at the last Space Shuttle launch at the Kennedy Space Center. A weekend at Arrowhead . . . She saw this room two weeks ago, David explaining that there was something she had to do; her not believing him. Dave saying he would go on a fishing trip and return in two weeks.

Lorena remembered taking Sherry to lunch for her birthday and their trip to London. It was too much. Her thoughts blurred. She felt consciousness slipping away. Through the fog she heard Dave's voice. "Lorena, please! It's okay. Everything's okay."

Chapter 33

The buzzy ringtone of "You Got to Have Friends" woke Sherry. Lorena never called this early. Something must be wrong. She rolled over and fumbled for the phone.

"Sherry, you're back!" Lorena caroled. "How was your trip?"

"Lorena." Sherry's voice was husky with sleep and the effect of a weeping jag. "You should have stayed it was . . . amazing." Memory blurred and refocused. "But that's right. You had to get back because Dave was coming home. How was his trip?"

"Um . . ." Lorena's voice sounded odd. "Sherry, exactly what do you remember?"

Sherry's mind blipped. Was her brain misfiring? "This is weird. I must have had a strong dream. Because in the dream, David had died a long time ago. I remember going to the funeral." She felt disoriented. "But that's not real?"

"Sherry, I need to see you right now. Can I come over?"

Sherry took the phone with her into the bathroom and caught a glimpse of herself in the mirror. "Oh lord," she muttered.

"Is something wrong?" Lorena's voice sounded worried.

Sherry looked away from her mascara-streaked reflection. "No. Nothing is wrong, and yes, you can come over. Give me thirty minutes. Bring Starbucks. A triple latte."

"You got it. See you." The phone clicked.

Sherry turned on the shower and lifted her face gratefully into the hot spray. The memory of her last time in this shower came like a wave of sweet pain. She blanked it and continued to wash her hair. She stroked on a minimum of makeup and slipped into her favorite navy sweats. She shivered. It was too cold to leave her hair wet. She turned on the blow dryer and finger combed her hair.

The doorbell rang. Drat! She grabbed her hairbrush as she ran to the front door. "That was not thirty min . . ." She dropped the hairbrush. All thought left her head

Jeremy stood there wearing a tan windbreaker and a blue sweater the color of his eyes.

It wasn't possible. Was she hallucinating? Sherry clutched the doorknob to keep herself upright.

Jeremy caught her in his arms and kissed her roughly. "Do you have any idea what you did to me when you left?"

Sherry pulled back and cupped his face with shaking hands. He looked much fitter than the last time he'd come through the door. His hair was just as silver, but he radiated strength and vitality. "You came," she whispered. "You didn't go through the door?"

"Hell, yes, I came through the door. Right after I figured out how to calibrate it past the day you returned."

"I don't understand." She wanted to hold him and never let him go.

"I'd forgotten how green your eyes were." He smoothed away the crease between her eyebrows. "It's a rather long story. May I come in?"

"Of course." She gripped his hand tightly and led him into the dining room.

He stopped dead at the sight of the two cups and the uneaten quiche. "I timed it right. I'm getting rather good at this."

Sherry picked up the dishes and put them in the sink. "I just got back last night and . . ." her voice broke, "I thought you'd think I didn't care enough to come back to you."

"You couldn't come back to me. I know that now. I invented the time machine." Jeremy sat down, his eyes never leaving her face. "I tried to come to you. My first trip to find you was by plane. I flew to Los Angeles in 1998. When I arrived at your shop, you were elsewhere."

His words buzzed in her head. "But I'm always here. When did you come?"

"September 1998."

Sherry thought back. "That's when the boys and I drove cross country to Maine for John's freshman year at Bates."

"So your store manager told me. I stayed in Los Angeles for a month, hoping you'd return." His lips quirked into the crooked smile she loved. "While I was here, I bought the land where The Castle sits."

Her mouth opened in shock. "*You* own The Castle?"

Jeremy nodded. "That's why Eric looked at me strangely when I asked to tour the computer that day. He probably thought it was some kind of test. I'm the one who hired him."

"This is so . . ." Sherry couldn't find words.

"I know." Jeremy traced her lips with his finger. "I tried again in April 2006. You were gone again."

Sherry tried to think past the deliciously abrasive feel of his fingertip. "April 2006? I was in Michigan for John's wedding."

"I tried again in November 2006. You were in Sacramento with Michael." Jeremy reached for her hand. "I finally realized I couldn't circumvent time. I couldn't change the future and neither could you. You couldn't come back to me that day and I couldn't come to you until you returned from 1969."

She stood frozen trying to take it all in. He pulled his hand back. "Sorry."

Her breath expelled. "No." She reached out and pulled him to her. "No." She lifted her face for his kiss.

He cupped his hands behind her head. "Are you sure?"

"Yes, I am sure." She wrapped her arms around him. "I have never been surer of anything in my life."

The kiss went on forever. Searching, reaching, remembering, and settling in to a new pattern.

A car horn honked.

"Lorena. What rotten timing." Sherry started down the steps. "Stay here," she ordered. "I'll head her off at the pass." She ran to Lorena's car.

"I brought bagels, too." Lorena beamed. "Am I good or what?"

"Now is not a good time." Sherry reached the coffee and the bagel bag. "Thanks for the coffee. Call me tomorrow. Maybe Jeremy and I can have dinner with you two."

Lorena's mouth dropped open. "Jeremy? From London? He's here?"

Sherry nodded.

Lorena looked past Sherry. Her eyes widened at the sight of Jeremy, now silver haired, waiting on the porch. "That's the most romantic thing I ever heard. Spill it," she ordered.

Sherry reached over and turned on the ignition for Lorena. "Goodbye. Call me tomorrow."

Sherry went back in the house and closed and locked the door. "Loot," she said, holding up the bags.

"I should have thought of that," Jeremy said.

"Never mind." She put the bags down and went back into his arms. "You'll stay?" Sherry asked when they finally pulled apart.

"If you want me."

"Don't be stupid. How long?"

Jeremy looked a little hesitant. "Well at some point I have to go back to London."

Sherry picked up the coffee and headed for the dining room. "Of course," she said, willing her voice not to break. "I don't know what I was thinking. You must have a family to get back to. I understand."

"No," Jeremy said. "You don't." He took the coffee from her and set it on the table. He turned her into his arms and buried his face in her hair. "Bloody Christ, Sherry, it's been so long. Sometimes I thought I'd never see you again."

Sherry heard the huskiness in his voice. She reached up and massaged the back of his neck.

His arms tightened around her. When he lifted his head, his eyes were wet. "After I realized you weren't coming back, I stayed drunk for a week. It didn't help. After a while, I started doing what you asked me to do. I lived those years."

"That's what I hoped you'd do." She ached to erase the sadness on his face. "So how many future stories did you end up printing?"

"None of them. I couldn't take a chance that I might change the future and never be able to find you again." He sat down at the table and pulled her into his lap. "I started researching time. I had an advantage, of course. I knew it could be done. I didn't expect it to take thirty two years." His eyes darkened with remembered frustration. "I had to wait until so many things were invented."

Sherry ran a wondering hand down his cheek. "I can't believe you invented a time machine."

"They say 'necessity is the mother of invention.'" His arms tightened around her. "You, my love, are my necessity."

She lifted her face for his kiss and saw the shadow in his eyes. "What's wrong?"

Jeremy turned away to pick up the latte, then put it down and looked at her squarely. "I would like to tell you I was faithful to your memory all that time, but I'd be lying. Eventually the loneliness caught up and I got married."

"I'm glad," Sherry said, stifling a pang of jealousy. "It's what I'd hoped for you. I didn't want you to go through life alone."

"The marriage lasted two years. It was a mistake. I didn't have that much to give her. But," his voice hardened, "Laura didn't care. My money was enough. She found a better meal ticket and left."

Jeremy smoothed Sherry's tight lips into a smile. "She gave me a gift though. She left me our daughter."

"A daughter," repeated Sherry softly. "What is her name? How old is she?

"Thirty two and her name is Kathryn. She's expecting her first child. I have to go back for that and I want you to come with me. Wherever we are, whatever we do from now on, it is together." Jeremy trailed a line of kisses down past her ear. "I've got my miracle back and I never want to let her go."

Sherry closed her eyes, reveling in the feel of his lips. She breathed in the unique fragrance that was purely Jeremy. "Forever. And no more time trips."

Jeremy's lips lingered at the nape of her neck. "I don't know about that," he murmured between kisses. "It might be fun for a little vacation. How do you feel about visiting Italy in the Renaissance?"

"Wonderful . . ." It was hard to think past the kisses. "And how would we do that? When Lorena and I went back our bodies grew younger. Exactly how old would we be in the fourteenth century?"

"Around twenty. It seems one can't be regressed past the age of physical maturity." His lips settled, feather light, over hers. "I tested it by going back to 1939 to see my parents as teenagers."

"Inspired, no doubt, by *Back to The Future?*" Sherry managed to say. The warmth of his breath made havoc of her thoughts.

"Of course." Jeremy lifted Sherry to her feet. "Forever is a long time. Perhaps we ought to begin it."

Her soul echoed the yearning in his eyes. "Yes." Sherry took his hand. "Now would be the perfect time for that." She led him upstairs.

Epilogue

The last rays of sunlight slanted through the bougainvillea, dappling gold shadows on the patio. Lorena leaned back in a green striped lounge chair and nibbled on a Brie covered cracker. "I don't see why we can't go back to Shakespeare's time again," she said with lips in full pout. "I only got to see one play."

"And almost got us burned as witches," Dave reminded her. "Anyway it's my turn to choose." He popped open a beer and moved Lorena's legs off the chaise so he could sit with her. "Ever since I saw *Midnight in Paris*, I've wanted to go back to the 1920's. Imagine meeting Hemingway!"

Jeremy flipped the salmon over with the confidence of a seasoned chef. "Might be fun." He took the platter of vegetables Sherry held out and smiled down at her. Their eyes held a conversation. After four years together they didn't need words.

"Paris would be lovely," Sherry agreed. "Think of the clothes."

"I wouldn't mind meeting Cole Porter," Lorena said.

Jeremy tipped the vegetables onto the grill. "I'd like to drive one of those Peugeot limos. Or perhaps a Duesenberg."

"Why do you always buy things you can't take home?" Lorena asked.

Jeremy's eyes followed Sherry as she set plates around the table. "I don't need souvenirs. I have everything I want right here."

They'd gotten married twice. Once in California

for Sherry's friends and family, and again in England for Jeremy's family.

Sherry had been a little intimidated by her first sight of his parents' castle in Sussex, but their warm welcome dispelled her misgivings.

Jeremy's mother and father loved Jeremy's time travel device. Now in their mid-nineties, they still took three or four trips a year. They said the trips kept them young.

"They're right, you know," Jeremy told Sherry after a strenuous tennis game with his father. "Time travel seems to be a tonic. I don't feel like I'm growing older." He mopped his brow as he watched his father stride briskly back to the castle. "One of these days I'm going to beat him."

Sherry thought love was the tonic. Every time he walked into the room, her heart filled with joy. She pulled his head down to hers. "Are you in the mood for a little more exercise?"

Jeremy's lips curved. "I don't believe I ever showed you our castle's secret passage. It leads right to our bedroom. Come on."

Sherry opened a London branch of *Now and Then* and made Jen the manager. Jennifer gave up acting after marrying her third husband. Their marriage was now in its tenth year and Jen seemed supremely happy. "Third time's the charm," she told Sherry in private.

Sherry laughed. "I think two's my magic number."

She and Jeremy spent six months of the year in London so they could be close to Kathryn and Daniel and baby Abigail. Three-year-old Abby had already dismantled a computer and three cell phones. Kathryn was sure she was going to be an inventor like Jeremy.

"More likely a surgeon," Jeremy remarked. "You should be grateful she's limiting herself to inanimate objects."

"I worry more about the fact that Abby calls every man she meets Daddy," Jen said, looking up from the inventory program Jeremy had installed on her laptop. "You don't want her taking after Great Aunt Jen."

The only one of the younger generation to time travel was Michael. Kathryn detested the idea. John and Janie wanted to wait till the twins were older. "A lot older," muttered Sherry exhausted by a day of chasing them around the park. "Maybe when they graduate college."

"Paris it is." Jeremy looked at Lorena. "What are you planning to tell Dylan this time?"

Ever since Dylan found the rapier Dave brought back from the sixteenth century, he'd been asking a lot of questions.

"I'm going to tell him I've rented a villa in Spain where we plan to celebrate our anniversary in the most intimate way possible. He'll wince and say, 'Ew! Too much information!' and that will be the end of it."

Lorena snuggled up beside him. "You're a genius. Although, he's sure to want us to bring back a bullfighter cape and matching sword."

"No problem. I did rent the villa," Dave whispered in her ear, "for the week after we come back."

Sherry looked at them wonderingly. "Do you suppose after forty years of marriage, we would still kiss like it's the first time?"

Jeremy drew Sherry into his arms. "With any luck at all," he whispered against her lips, "we have a very good chance of finding out."

www.ingramcontent.com/pod-product-compliance
Lightning Source LLC
Chambersburg PA
CBHW072352190626
46811CB00019B/556